Further praise for *Unspec*

"A beautifully woven st[...]
juggle from ourselves and others... *Unspectacular* reveals a profound
truth about our modern society. Relatable, engaging, and wonderfully
nuanced... a compelling tale for those pondering their place in the world."

- Michael Lauer, novelist and touring guitarist

"So good... Vivid characters and storytelling."

- Krista Wax, Host at KFAI Radio

"Incredibly convincing. I was especially attached to Mae... a great job
balancing an ensemble cast while pushing a few voices to the front...
jarring-in-a-good way... really fun to read."

- Sofie Riley, novelist and singer-songwriter

Further excerpts from *Louder Than War* magazine

"A compelling debut novel that intricately explores the struggles of
adulthood, self-discovery, and the pursuit of creative and personal
aspirations.... *Unspectacular* captures the beauty and messiness of
pursuing one's passions while grappling with the realities of adulthood.

"Through its multiple perspectives, the novel delves into themes of
family, ambition, and cultural identity. Baker's sharp prose and biting
humour create an engaging narrative that paints a vivid picture of
modern challenges, from societal pressures to internal conflicts. [Baker]
also writes in such a way that the reader can relate to the characters
and feel a great amount of empathy for them. Fans of contemporary
and psychological fiction will find Baker's exploration of these themes
both thought-provoking and emotionally resonant. Baker's storytelling
reminds us that even in life's chaos, there's beauty in finding our path."

Also by Zaq Baker

Albums

If It's Not Zaq Baker Live at the Green Room, I'm Not Going (2023)

Solarbaby (2023)

This Time It's Personal (2022)

Maddie's Delivery Service (2021)

Cardio (2020)

Getting Younger (2018)

Housewarming (2017)

Standalone singles

"theatre girls will break your heart" (feat. Corzine) (2024)

"spearmint" [neon redux] (2024)

"jetlag" (feat. Maria Coyne) (2024)

"treadmill" (feat. Corzine) (2024)

"Nervous (Anne's Audition Song)" (feat. Anne Brown) (2023)

"Molly's Song" (The Woes of Marketing for an American National Dairy Farming Subsidiary Best Known for Exporting Milk Products, e.g., Cream, Cottage Cheese, Yogurt and Other Novelties) (2021)

"Cavemen" (2021)

"Ojos" (2021)

"Never Getting Older" (2021)

Published creative writing

"After the Last Midtown Show" (*Vagabond City*)

"Strangers: Cricket and the Passage of Time" (*The Alternative*)

Concept music videos

"Get the Message"

"Someone to Believe In"

"I Wanna Be Your Night Owl"

"Spearmint"

Live videos

If It's Not Zaq Baker Live at the Green Room, I'm Not Going (collection)

Good Kid Manic Summer (collection: "Down for Whatever" and "She's Nocturnal")

Unspectacular was written, published, and obsessed over in the United States of America, primarily in its middle north. First printed in 2025.

Unspectacular is a work of fiction. Names, characters, places, and incidents are the products of the author's overactive imagination. Any resemblance to actual rock venues, hijinx, schools and offices (drab or otherwise), careers (failed or otherwise), or persons, living or dead, is entirely coincidental.

© Zachary Baker 2025

ISBN: 979-8-9920384-0-8

Library of Congress Control Number: 2024924847

unspectacular

a novel
zaq baker

Emily —

Thank you so much
for supporting this
dream — and I hope
you enjoy this
music story ♥

Zaq
BAKER

February 15<u>th</u>, 2024 (a Thursday)
Mae

I can feel everything in my body, and it's awful.

That little space between your eyebrows — somehow mine hurts. I didn't even know that was possible until this morning. It must be from frowning. There's also a hard, wet lump in my throat that no amount of swallowing will make go away. And the ringing in my ears is unstoppable.

Last night my mother... well, more on last night in a second. She wants me to record an album that, in Robert's words, will make use of my "natural talents" and "high potential." Lately she's been pressuring me to "research" artists in town so I can "get [my] own act together." The idea of working on this album is terribly unpleasant, and the process hasn't even started yet. Oppressive. It would be a stressor, too, if I was putting in a crumb of labor. But I'm not. I won't.

But even with all her coercion, Ingrid won't accompany me on excursions like yesterday's. She says that's because she wants me to "develop independence" and "show [her] some initiative." She has her own reasons for staying home, but she won't open up to me about it. I know exactly where her limits are, and that's one of them.

⌢

Trying to make good on Ingrid's assignment, I'd forgotten to bring my ID to Genuine Failures Club, a venue that's aptly named and situated about fifteen minutes away from our house by train. The card shouldn't have been a problem; misplaced identity or not, I was only going to get a glass of water. But the bouncer turned me away at the door. "Got to have a wristband," he grunted. Then, though I'm certain we'd never met, he looked at me with a strange curiosity, almost like he recognized me. This happens to me once in a while, more often since my teenage years, which I'm still not quite sure I've left behind. The security guard was probably in his late forties or early fifties. After that, he just shrugged and ushered me out into the light snow outside.

Underage, under-awning, failing genuinely and watching the flakes fall, I figured I'd much rather lie to my mother, which I have loads of experience doing, than admit to her I didn't even make it inside. I decided quickly to sneak in through Genuine Failures' side door: the load-in entrance, marked PERFORMER USE ONLY. You can slink inside and feign you belong as long as you compose the right look on your face when someone hauling an amp or merchandise or components of a drum kit swings the door open for a second or two. All you have to do is pretend to be a musician. That's what I've been doing my whole life.

Sometimes I'll bring a backpack and homework — music theory worksheets from Grimm's Academy, where I'm more or less a college sophomore. This way people assume I'm busy, which discourages them from looking at me funny for being alone. Every few visits I make, though, someone the bouncer's age will start playing that same game, the one I don't understand. Walking over to my table, where I've made it obvious I'd like to be by myself, they'll peer at me, sort of smiling, sort of frowning, and say, "I swear I recognize you from somewhere."

I don't get it. Being honest — with strangers — I'll shrug and shake my head, demure, and make a point of the solitude I've chosen by gesturing vaguely toward the books in front of me. I don't have enough inklings there to maintain a proper conversation. Plus, I don't want to. It's not my job to entertain them.

Robert Koenid, Esquire, came into our lives on a Tuesday in September, a little over four months ago and the second day of my current school year at Grimm's. That day, Robert had been guest-lecturing as an entertainment lawyer — thank god he doesn't *work* at the music school where I'm forced to show up several times a week — and kept me after class once he'd heard me speak. All I'd done was introduce myself, and only then because it was required, but Robert insisted that I confer with him privately at the desk the Academy had set up for his visit. He said he was charmed by my vocal tone. I wasn't even singing, but after I'd given my name, just two syllables, he said he wanted very much to hear more. He also noted my "aggressively Scandinavian" features, telling me my "natural aesthetic" and vocal gifts would take me far. Sharpness, Robert informed me, "below-average height notwithstanding," is always in vogue in the industry. Did he ask me whether making it in the music business is something I'm keen on doing? No. But that day Robert proceeded to explain: there's always electropop, "time-honored for performers of my visual and hereditary ilk," or, if that's not my bag, "the more contemporary, boundary-pushing world of indie," dominated by "bloodlines from [my] part of the world." Can you imagine why I'm not interested in making music with this guy?

But now Robert lives in our house. I don't remember my actual dad — not my fault; Erik Strand passed on, I'm told, when I was very small. He'd been walking to the pet society from our family home to take a first look at an abandoned puppy. Passing under the shadow of some Chicago apartment complex, Erik was halfway to the shelter when a piano plummeted directly toward him from the top floor — six hundred pounds of wood and ivory dropped from twenty stories up, straight onto his head. A group of movers had been easing the upright down when they lost control of the belay grips or the cable system or whatever, and the beautiful machine rocketed to the ground. Erik was killed instantly. He literally had to face the music while stepping out to see a man about a dog.

I can't guess how much Erik's death impacted Ingrid's transformation into a complete recluse, which she's been as far back as I can remember. Or maybe she's always been a depressed person, a deflated type, a phantom. How should I know?

Genuine Failures is seldom crowded, probably because no one who performs there is very famous or very good. Last night, having crept my way to a corner table, I found myself half-watching a solo act in his late twenties finish a rock cover to tepid applause. Then, to my horror, he made eye contact. With me.

I hadn't been sitting down long enough to hide behind my academy packets. From my vantage in the back, I'd figured I was invisible.

"You look like a singer," he slurred, unprompted. *Why?*, I wondered, heart pounding. "Open mic. You've gotta get up here and do a song!"

Who dares attack my privacy? Maybe he was drunk. Maybe my "perma-scowl" (credit: Ingrid) struck this guy as a moody artist's go-to. Maybe my "elfin elements" (credit: Robert) struck the performer as... I don't know. Vulnerable? Secretly fierce? That's how I see myself, anyway. Maybe it was what my mother calls my calico — a very intentional streak of jet black in my light tawny hair, the only thing other than my age that sets me apart visually from her. I suppose Ingrid is taller than me, too. People named Ingrid usually are. Maybe my style came across as artistic or *alternative*. (When people say that, I often wonder: alternative to what?)

In any case, having people project their ideas onto you is exhausting. At the G.F.C. performer's invitation, which felt more like an accusation, I felt my stomach churn and sink, quicker than an average panic, an anchor heaving inside me.

It's easy for me to lie to my mom, and I can pull it off with Robert most of the time, so why is it so hard with people I don't know?

"Cat got your tongue?"

I must've sat there without saying or doing anything for longer than I thought, because the guy on stage looked at me funnier than I'm used to — first in disbelief at my silent refusal, then in surprise at my total frozenness, and ultimately with a weird sort of pity. As he began to noodle on his guitar again, I can't say what made it finally happen: my failure to produce a smooth lie, or my actual fear at jumping on stage, even in a mostly empty bar. But it happened fast. I felt a hard tug upward on that anchor just before a mass of seaweed lurched free and gave way to a warm rush moving upward toward my throat through my ribcage.

No, I found myself pleading inward and nearly praying outward — then, more firmly: *no*.

But the happening was out of my hands. Before conscious thought could kick in, I bolted upward from the table, covering my mouth, still soundless, and darted all the way to the front door. No need, thankfully, to shimmy and shove past a bouncer from the inside. I thrust the aperture back open, ran out into the snowy night, doubled over, and vomited into the evergreen.

February 15th (the same morning)
Mae

"Up."

My mother has entered my room without my permission. She has also cranked the dysfunctional blinds as far as they can go, bringing an unwelcome splash of sunlight alongside her.

If she expects me to respond verbally, I don't.

I cover my head.

"Rise," she says.

Grandiose, I think, *but I never see you leave the house.*

From under my pile of blankets, I can hear Ingrid fidgeting with the shades and trying to fix them, but I know it won't work. She does this every few days, then gets frustrated, then forgets how aggravated she got. Then, like a housecat, she'll try it again later.

"You've got a theory lesson with Emily in a few hours," I hear her say.

My mother is enjoying a very rare burst of energy — probably because *I* have things to do.

"What's the point of doing my own music if I can't cancel at the last minute anyway?" My voice sounds ghastly, hopefully because I've only been awake for a few seconds, but the scratchiness still appalls me. Still buried in pillows, I'm hoping Ingrid can't pick apart my tone at this level of muffle. And if I continue to refuse to move, I don't have to look at her, and she can't see me.

She does, though. "Robert isn't going that easy on you. Plus, he and I want to hear about Genuine Failures last night — what happened, what you learned."

That anchor in my stomach lurches again. Last night I'd been so focused on keeping down nausea on the train ride home, I'd forgotten to stitch something convincing together for the pair of them. Thoroughly dizzy, I'd collapsed pretty much the moment I'd returned, at least as I remember it. Good thing Ingrid sleeps all the time. I was right to assume she'd have fallen asleep or disappeared completely by the time I got here. And who knows what Robert was doing?

I moan involuntarily.

"You don't smell good," my mother says, more sharply than before. I can practically see her eyes narrow. "Did you *drink* last night?"

I decide quickly to play up my offense, which is sincere. Living in Ingrid and Robert's house, under their rules, I've got to take all the bargaining power I can get. "Can we not with the accusations today?"

She repeats the question. I can nearly hear a pointless *when I was your age*, but she decides not to draw it. That sort of condescension is more Robert's speed.

"Not on my life," I tell her. There's a solace in clinging to one truth, even a small one. I debate poking my head out of the blankets to show her I mean it... but I don't.

Ingrid exhales heavily. "There's a whole day ahead of you, Mayfly. If you're not downstairs in five minutes..." I wait for a stock maternal phrase — *so help me* or *it's curtains for you, young lady*, or even *there'll be hell to pay*, but her leverage over me isn't that major. My singing voice is like magic to her. It's almost supernatural. On the rare occasions she deigns to encourage or protect me, it's for that reason. Robert is the intimidating one around here. Ingrid and I both know she would never try *when you're finally out of this house* and would rather let *wait til Robert hears about this* unfold on its own.

Still, my mother can apply psychological pressure like no one else. It's funny: her bits of guidance, which are as infrequent as they are random, suggest she knows *some*thing about the business of music. How difficult it is to secure a living, for example. Who will screw you. How quickly stars can rise, and, more importantly, how rapidly they fade. But she gets awfully quiet when it comes to the mechanics: scales, breathing, posture, technique. Quieter still if you ask about her life before I showed up. Probably the knowledge comes from Robert. Anyway, I haven't tried prodding that barrier in a long time. I'm saving that moment for when I really need to lash out.

"How long til my lesson with Emily?"

There's no response. I push the pillows aside and lift my head to see nothing where I'd expected Ingrid to be hovering over me. Maybe her good mood has dissipated already. I wouldn't be surprised. She moves so silently these days I didn't even realize she'd gone.

Sitting alone at the breakfast table, I'm making a show of staring at my music theory homework in case anyone comes downstairs. I have to meet with my Emily in a few hours so she can instruct me. I wish I understood the assignment. Diminished chords? Add-eleven? They're only blots of ink on staff paper. It all feels like a mess to me.

Ingrid appears, yawning, in an all-white bathrobe. She has emerged from her secretive upper quarters to cross through the doorframe like it's a suburban torii gate. She's also pretending she didn't invade my room five minutes ago, interrogate me, and demand that I start the day.

"What are you doing, baby?"

"Today's homework assignment, Mom," I issue through a scowl. "We literally just talked about it."

Ingrid crosses to the kitchen and begins to prepare a pot of coffee. "Tell me about the show last night."

Robert enters the room in a dress shirt and slacks. I rarely see him in anything other than a stereotypical lawyer uniform. He's breathing heavily, almost always is. His tie is draped loosely around his neck, and he's holding something behind his back.

For a moment I enjoy a private sigh, relieved at the chance to avoid fabricating last night's failed G.F.C. experience to my mother. I return to my homework assignment while Robert presents a small jewelry box to Ingrid. She opens it, now holding a necklace in one hand and almost pawing at it with the other.

Robert smiles. "Things have been going well with Chyrons."

"Semi-retired," Ingrid says through another yawn. "Right." She sets the box on the counter and adjusts Robert's tie.

"Got another meeting in the city this morning," he says.

"I'll be here, admiring my new chain."

I continue to scribble in my music theory book as Robert putters around the kitchen self-importantly, getting ready for his day.

"What's the assignment?" Ingrid asks me.

I don't like being triangulated between Ingrid and Robert, but with her near the table and him pouring coffee, I'm sort of stuck here.

"Um." I turn the worksheet toward her on the table. "You're supposed to circle the middle of this triad, add the voicing, and name the chord."

Ingrid studies the staff paper and, unshockingly, points out a flaw in my work. "This is a minor chord, honey. You wrote 'major'."

"Well, I don't think they should be called 'minor.' It's demeaning."

"It's important they're phrased differently, baby. They're supposed to sound sad."

You sound sad, I think, but I say nothing. She drifts across the room and out of my view into the vestibule in the hall, then decides to call from the other room: "You still haven't told us how it was at Genuine Failures, honey. Did you even go?"

I swear I sense a change in my mother's mood, that she isn't completely kidding. I must wait too long to respond, because she reënters the room and turns toward me.

"Why don't you tell us what *really* happened last night?"

I drop my pen, which clatters on the table as I try to compose myself.

Robert, as usual, is trying too hard to play the part of the dad — and, based on what classmates have told me, he's nailing it: the man is so invested in his business life that social goings-on at home slip past him completely. "Did I miss something?"

Ingrid just looks at me, eyebrows cocked.

"Well, I really did go to Genuine Failures Club," I manage.

Ingrid presses her index and middle fingers against her eyes. She looks directly at Robert as if to urge: *say something.*

Robert shrugs.

Ingrid: "You weren't sneaking drinks, were you? Anything illicit?"

"House spirits," Robert suggests.

The real house spirit is Ingrid, floating around here, shuttered in the building by her own design. Though the liquid comments are false, I remain silent. It's easier that way.

"I thought you'd have more concern for our d — for my daughter."

"Robert," I interpose under my breath, "is more of a roommate."

Ingrid simply stares at me, eyes narrowed, then throws her hands up. "You know what? I cannot deal with this. I'm going back to bed."

She exits.

Robert, arms folded, faces me. "What happened?"

I hunch my shoulders defensively, still avoiding eye contact. "I dunno. I caught a bit of music last night, and then I got sick, so I left."

"You got sick."

Suddenly, I feel something bad — something I recognize right away. "Oh, god."

"What?"

I stand up. "It's happening again." I bolt out of the room and sort of just hang there in the hall, avoiding Robert. From the kitchen, I can still hear him invading my space by giving me music advice.

"Your lesson is at eleven," he calls, voice raised. "I'm taking the car. You'd better be ready to take the train in an hour." I don't respond. "You're not going to miss this lesson because *you* did something that displeased your mother. I refuse to pay the cancellation fee." I can hear self-satisfaction from across the house: "Maybe there's another lesson there."

Still, I don't respond.

"You'd better have something prepared for your teacher," he adds.

And still — I don't respond.

February 15th (a few hours later)
Mae

Emily is endlessly, achingly sincere, which makes it very difficult to lie to her. You can hear her genuineness in her questions, that she's legitimately interested in what you have to say. That she listens when you respond. I think that's rare in people. I've never once seen her pull her phone out when I'm speaking, even when we're jockeying with our calendars at the end of "session." (That's her word for lessons. She really does run them like therapy.)

You can also see the sympathy in Emily's eyes, which carry so much fatigue you want someone to tell her to set everyone else' baggage down, just for a minute. She's only a decade or two older than me, maybe in her thirties, but you can see little half-moon depressions of purplish-black underneath each of her lower lids. She's tallish and freckled, brimming with an optimism and an instilled resilience that makes me feel old by comparison.

This morning Emily has been teaching someone much younger and even more amateurish than I am. Level-one guidebooks are splayed across the keybed, each adorned with a wide range of brightly colored stickers. All of them are shaped like stars.

"Every Good Boy Does Fine," she recites as she folds the sheet of staff paper and sets it aside. She looks coy. "Not always true, is it?"

Already, in her kindness, Emily has put me at a crossroads. I don't want to admit I haven't prepared for our session, so joining in her playfulness might buy me a little time. That said, I've always been very hesitant to share much of my interior life with anyone — probably because Robert and Ingrid have been so over-involved. Plus, boys have never interested me. Girls don't either. Sometimes I'm afraid nothing does.

As at Genuine Failures, I've found a shrug helps me dodge personal questions, a method I try to use once per session. That's my personal limit. I think more would have me hurting her feelings.

I'm so in my head this morning I forget to actually shrug, which Emily does in response to the silent time lapse. Small score: I can harvest my one shoulder motion for later.

"Okay," she says gently. "What's on your mind today, Mayfly?"

Other than my mother, Emily is the only person who calls me that. Perhaps they share a sense of limited time. That's what mayflies are, right? Short-lived? Either way, the phrase makes me feel like a kid, which I detest coming from my mother but which Emily makes warm and encouraging.

Here's the thing: I sing strictly for pleasure, and even then, I'm not sure how much bliss I get out of it. I don't enjoy *work*ing on my voice, and I definitely don't want to be famous or influential or recognized or, frankly, heard by other people. Sometimes with Emily it's alright, but I prefer to keep to myself. Robert, on the other hand, is fixated on my prospects for being a "mover and shaker" in the music industry, which only makes me resist the idea more. Ingrid is right there with him, brightening at my "poise for success" without thinking about what *I* might want. Or don't want. Being unspectacular is fine with me.

I avoid looking up at Emily. Evading the truth, especially by capitalizing on Emily's interest in me, feels close enough to lying that it stirs remorse, and a twinge of this morning's nausea rears its head again.

I stare at another leaf of staff paper, where Emily has labeled the bass clef mnemonic for beginners: *All Cows Eat Grass.*

Time to stall. "Well, I think I could get more music done," I hear myself saying, "if it wasn't for factors outside my control."

In my hesitation, I drag out "well" at the front, and it sounds, idiotically, like "wool." I steal a glance at Emily, who's sitting dangerously close to me. She likes to share the piano bench. She says this is so she can walk students through exercises together, but I think she simply likes sharing... which is not an inclination I understand.

But Emily isn't looking at me; she knows directness makes me uncomfortable. "What d'you mean?" she asks. She's probably cocking her head a little. When she does this, you can practically see her ears perk up like one of those emotionally intelligent sheepdogs. Sometimes I wonder whether Emily knows how easily she pulls people into her orbit. The habit seems natural, though. With her, everything does.

"Pressure," I say. "It's holding me back."

It occurs to me I'm telling the truth. I peek sidelong at Emily again, and her eyes are wide open, saturnine, a swell of apologies almost bursting out of her. She thinks it's her fault.

"Wool, not from *you*," I blurt. "From my mom. Robert too."

"Would you like to talk about your mom? About that pressure?"

Even though both options are bad, I decide I'd rather open up about my home life than about my lack of homework progress since last Thursday. Talking to Emily really does help anyway. "Wool... my mom and Robert say they're so *invest*ed in me. But my mom feels like more of a *presence* than an *influence*. Like, my whole life, she's wanted me to do well in this vague way, so big and so broad it's kind of taken over everything, even though she's never really said anything about it. Not til recently. And Robert only wants me to do well because he's obsessed with my mom and her happiness."

Emily frowns: the empathy literally pulls her face downward. I can tell she's refraining from putting her hand on my shoulder. "Or," I continue, "because he's a lawyer. Entertainment guy. Now they're both set on me recording an album before this winter's over so I can *make my mark*. So they can get some power in the world. Or money." I plink the middle *C* before me on the piano. "But I don't want to be their cash cow."

I'm still staring at the keybed, where little residual marks of glue have left five-point shapes over most of the middle and upper octaves — star stickers Emily must've once used to teach notes to her youngest students. Constellations of encouragement. The colors have all faded by now.

My mother once called me a *nihilist*. That was long before I'd hit an appropriate age to guess at what that meant. I still haven't looked it up, actually. The point is that she accused me, in a whisper, of *not believing in anything*. That charge has really stuck with me. But I can't help it, the not caring. And the older I get, the better I understand Ingrid was projecting herself, her shortcomings, onto a much smaller version of me.

"Really," Emily says softly.

I shrug, but it's a different kind than before, so I'm not counting it. "Wool... I never hear Ingrid sing or play at home, but I can *feel* her in the practice room when I'm in there."

"Like she's haunting it."

For the first time all session, I look directly at Emily, whose tired eyes have widened again. The hair on her arms is raised, too. Her concern and her trademark depth of interest have replaced her quickness to blame herself. I've said too much, probably.

"I don't want to talk about this anymore," I tell her.

Emily exhales. "You know everything here stays between us." She says it kind of like a clarifying question. For a second, her careful discretion reminds me of the pulmonologist my mom had me see when I was nine or ten, when, in Ingrid's view, I wasn't breathing deeply enough during vocal exercises. (I was fine.)

"I — " Emily says, then stops. "You know what, never mind."

"What?"

Emily smiles. "I feel like you *could* get more music done if you actually put the work in."

I groan. "You sound like my mom."

"*No* one sounds like your mom," Emily says with arresting certainty. I can nearly hear a *trust me*, but with Emily, that's hardly necessary. "Let's look at your progress since last week. Did you focus more on vocal exercises, music theory, or trying to compose?"

I wonder how many minutes are left in our session. I remember how I felt when I woke up this morning and figure I can use that to my advantage without, technically, lying.

"I don't feel so good," I say.

"You *happen* to be feeling sick, right when we're supposed to start reviewing your work?"

If you don't practice, it's no good to have a music teacher who actually pays attention to you. Now Emily's exhausted eyes suddenly feel a lot less like a border collie's and more like a pulsating pair of telescopes — astronomical, wide-ranging. Worse yet, I actually *do* feel a wave of nausea the moment she turns toward me, but there's nothing I can do to convince her it's real. I'm the girl who cried something like motion sickness.

"You are a bit pale," Emily concedes. She's being even gentler with me now, which only makes me feel worse. Staring down at the middle octaves, I make a slight movement that could be interpreted as shaking my head.

"Can we talk about something else?"

Emily sighs and checks her watch. Even in this bright room, the timepiece is backlit in green, its ticking rectangular numbers chunky and awkward. Dorky and scientific-looking, I bet it's a gift from some family member who doesn't understand how sensitive and understated Emily is. Or maybe that's my own imagination.

"Look," Emily says, "All I'll say is... that pressure you mentioned from your mom — and Robert — maybe you feel... hemmed in." Then she mumbles something, and it's unclear, but I think I hear *padlock*. "But... I don't know, Mayfly."

I cadge another glance, but Emily is staring down at the keybed, too, in a lower octave. On a weathered black note, you can just barely make out yellow adhesive where one of her stars used to stick.

"My mother," I say, confused, "a padlock."

The distinction takes a moment. "*Paddock.*" Smiling, Emily gestures toward a lullaby posted on the wall, where cartoon sheep are jumping over a cartoon fence. "Enclosure."

Gently she plods the a-minor-seven she named earlier today: *A, C, E, G.*

"So maybe," she continues, "pastures for you will always be greener on the other side. But no more games now." Even when she's being stern, Emily is still warm. "Let's hear what you've been working on."

I do have one reserve, stowed away for when my stalling has run out, and I'm not proud of this last ditch. Repressing a fresh bout of nausea, I start to root around in my backpack.

February 15th (the same Thursday) (but also February 9th) (a little bit)
(as explained)
Mae

Last Friday night, I was bringing Robert home in moderate snow from
some hotel bar when he insisted we stop so he could brush off the rear
window for me. I'd said I could see fine, but he said "a man has got to
look correctly if he's going to look backward." It's always these — *he,
him, his* — when Robert administers advice on the music business, his
only subject of conversation. He'll get more talkative coming home from
a "client meeting" at some bar downtown or an artist's place. Robert
says it's important for the aging attorney to "fortify his legal discussions
[with gin]," because "he has to uphold the role of his profession." When
nights like these wrap up, insistent on hoarding the money he'd otherwise
spend on a taxi home, he'll call Ingrid, who, being a lazy hermit, will
"ask" me to do it. I don't really have a choice. All three of us know that.

I shrugged and pulled the car onto the shoulder. Robert was wearing
a suit jacket with black tennis shoes and a Kane County Cougars baseball
cap. He looked like a businessman from an eighties movie or a divorcée
trying too hard to look cool. Or a retired ballplayer, the kind who used to
be fit and professionally successful and who now doles out guidance to
junior athletes or offers commentary on sports networks or something.

I've never seen Robert wear a winter coat. He says a good lawyer has
got to *embrace the cold*. I think this is stupid, but I don't say anything.
You can't just deflate a person like that.

So when Robert stepped out of the car, I figured he'd be a solid few minutes; he's big on thoroughness. Since my instinct for mild rebellion stretches beyond lying, I eyed his legal briefcase on the passenger seat and decided, just for fun, to take a look inside. The stack of papers was topped with lyrics and staff notation, six or seven scans of each. If he practices copyright law, maybe a full band was reviewing transcriptions of the music. Who knows?

I glanced over my shoulder at the back windshield, where Robert was engrossed in scratching at the pane. Unable to resist, I thumbed through the copies, licking the corners, took one of each, folded the two, and tucked them in my crimson jacket pocket.

I'd just shut the valise and set it back on the seat when the passenger door opened and Robert, powdered head to toe in fresh flurry, stepped back inside. He didn't shake the snow off his shoes. "I can get the car messy," he said, "because it's mine."

I rolled my eyes as Robert set the briefcase on the dash. Glancing at it while he buckled his seatbelt, I felt a swift twinge of nausea, but when I turned my gaze back to the windshield and watched the pane defrost, the feeling went away. I chalked the ill sensation up to the gin wafting from the passenger side. Sloughing off the feeling, I put the car in drive.

"*Mae*," says Emily, more firmly this time. She waves a *hello* from across the piano bench, where an open book of children's music from a prior lesson — "Baa Baa Black Sheep" on one page, "Twinkle Twinkle Little Star" on the next — is spread out between us. "Where'd you go?"

She says this to me when I drift off, which is often. I associate attention with pressure — can you imagine why? — but never Emily's.

"Did you write something for this week?" she says, gently. Even though it's always warm in this room, Emily is wearing a vest, and one of its top corners is turned upward, like the ear of a puppy. She says the temperature is part of piano care, but I think she just likes comfort.

"Yeah," I murmur. "Let me find it..." Both sheets of the song I plucked from Robert's briefcase are still stashed in the pocket of my cardinal coat, which is balled up in the corner.

Rooting around for the papers, I realize with a jolt I never even looked at them. This means I'm going to have to sightread and sing the lyrics and the staff paper in real time. I'm no good at that. Plus, full tilt, my headache has reared again.

It's a good thing the lyric sheet is typed, because Emily is the type of person who would remember my handwriting and question the difference. Heart pounding, I set the sheets on the keybed, one next to the other. I squint at the staff paper, then the lyrics, hoping desperately Emily isn't looking at either sheet of paper. I also hope she isn't looking at me. As long as I've known Emily, she's been able to hear — *feel* — every note. She doesn't need to see them.

I attempt to clear my throat, but the nausea has gravitated to my windpipe and feels like a locket strung too tight, or maybe a collar a kitten has outgrown. The result is more of a strained burp.

"Are you okay?"

I detect a tiny bit of resignation in Emily's tone and sneak a sidelong glance. She's reading the lyric sheet — actually paying attention to it. "You were going to sing," she says, sounding suddenly empty.

"Wool... yeah, I just. Um." I twiddle the corners of the staff paper closest to me.

"Mae..." Emily sighs. "If you were *any*one else."

How can she be upset? Does she recognize something I don't?

My locket/collar is growing tighter.

"If you didn't have *that* voice," she says. If I've got such a great voice, I'm not using it now.

Emily sucks in her breath, then sighs again. "Just... *please* do your homework next time." Now she's the one avoiding eye contact. "Because I'd really, really like to keep you around."

Our time's not up, but Emily gestures at the sheets of paper: *Here, you take these.* Sheepishly I gather them, then stuff my crimson coat under my arm. I'm not even going to wear it to the train station. Normally the heat in Emily's room is inviting, but now it's oppressive.

I stand up and start to turn the doorknob, which, here in Emily's tiny practice room, is right next to the piano. I'm standing in the frame when she says, "Hey," just as softly as she'd said my name before.

I turn, but I can't face her, so I fidget uselessly with the zipper on my cherry jacket.

"Just... tell your mom we did something constructive today."

Something in Emily's tone tells me this request is more a favor to Emily than it is a life raft for me, and I'm not sure why, but I nod, eager for anything to balance the scales. Robert himself once told me Grimm's Academy instructors are obligated to report or at least affirm progress to the parents of students there on loans from (in my case) The Bank Of Ingrid And Probably Robert. Or maybe he'd just said that to threaten me into practicing. I already feel like I owe Emily for being so patient and encouraging, not to mention letting happen whatever just happened, and, for reasons beyond me, not mentioning it to the pair of them.

"Okay," I squeak. The locket/collar is so tight by now I can barely pass vowels through it. For some reason it reminds me of the chain Robert gave Ingrid. Muted, I just nod again. Emily is already paging through a lesson planner for her next student, and I feel a pang of envy: she's thinking about someone else while I'm standing right there. In a way, I guess I'm as protective of Emily as she is of me.

I no longer trust my own voice to muster a "bye," so I do my best to direct some kind of meaningful expression at Emily. After all, I won't see her for another week. But she doesn't look up.

February 17<u>th</u> (a Saturday)
Mae

When trapped in the Strand living room or "family" vehicle, I often push down the pressure and tedium from Robert and Ingrid by picturing life as a TV show — a very unexciting one, and probably low-budget. My imagination gets set off by the combination of boredom and a lack of control. Tonight it's like this:

```
FADE IN on car interior. ROBERT is driving;
the passenger seat is empty. MAE is seated in
the back. Zipping past highway signs, the car
is approaching the outer limits of evening
CHICAGO. ROBERT is sporting his traditional
suit jacket and Kane County Cougars baseball
cap. MAE is shivering in her cherry winter
coat.


                    ROBERT
   I don't understand why you sit back there.


               MAE [sotto voce]
       I don't understand why you care.


                    ROBERT
                 What's that?
```

>   MAE
>   Nothing.

ROBERT is doing that annoying thing where the driver spends more time looking back at their passengers than at the road.

>   MAE [*accusatory*]
>   What?

>   ROBERT
>   Nothing.

They travel in silence for a full minute.

MAE mumbles a request to put music on.

>   ROBERT [*unhearing*]
>   What's that?

>   MAE *sighs*.
>   Nothing.

MAE pokes absently through the clutter of CD's littering the backseat, not recognizing or taking interest in any of the titles, monikers or cover artwork.

>   ROBERT
We're getting your mother a birthday present.

>   MAE
>   This far in advance? She's a Leo.

ROBERT
It's a surprise.

MAE
Why do I have to come?

ROBERT *[as if prepared]*
Would you rather buy your mother a gift with
your own funds? Or with a little fiscal boost
from Robert Koenid, Attorney at Law?

MAE rolls her eyes.

MAE
Semi-retired.

ROBERT
You drive me home from my meetings in the
city all the time. I thought it would be
nice for us to spend money on something
proper together. And it would make
your mother happy.

MAE stares out the window.

MAE
That last part is impossible.

ROBERT
I was thinking diamonds. Maybe pearls.

MAE
Must be nice, being a lawyer.

                    ROBERT
   Semi-retired, remember. And there's lots
   of fortune in the entertainment industry.
   Luck, I mean — that kind of fortune. Not the
   riches. Not necessarily. [*Long pause*] Anyway,
   your mother likes pretty things that become
              valuable under pressure.

They drive in silence.

                     MAE
Why did we have to come all the way out here?

ROBERT doesn't respond.

Several full minutes pass. By this point
the lengthy pauses should feel awkward to
our audience, but not for either party in
the car: ROBERT, a man of business with a
history around men in business, is accustomed
to stony silences — and MAE divides her
residence between her mother's house and her
own head, and maintains low expectations of
the adults around her. Well, except Emily.

The vehicle pulls up to a warehouse-looking
building.

                     MAE
           This is the jewelry shop?

ROBERT parks the car and shuts off the
engine, reminding our audience of his
imperviousness to the cold.

ROBERT
Look... I wanted to bring you to a place
that's special to me. And to your mother,
actually.

MAE
[...]

ROBERT
Inside that building is a studio — a real
one. I've worked with this producer,
Håvi Håvsstrom, many times. And now you're
going to work with him, too.

MAE
Wait — this is for the album you and Ingrid
have been pushing me about all the time?

ROBERT nods.

MAE
And now you're — making it into some
weird coming-of-age ritual?
Dragging me out here as a creepy surprise?

ROBERT [frustrated]
Look, I'm not going to tell you to be
grateful. But you should be. With your
talents, my acumen is a good thing for you.
And this — your mother and I are giving you a
good opportunity here.

MAE
By bringing me to some music industry
building without even telling me?

ROBERT
You are... vexingly private, Mae. Especially
with music. It makes your mother sad. And it
inhibits me from helping you be successful.
We figured if we told you about Håvi's
studio — that this is where we'd be going,
that you'd be trying things out here — you
wouldn't want to come.

MAE [*shaking her head*]
Oh my god.

ROBERT
What?

MAE [*angrily*]
I'm like a [*redacted*] housepet to you and
Ingrid. Is that what this is? You have to
trick me — like we're going to do something
fun so we can go to the [*redacted*] vet?

ROBERT [*huffing*]
You know what? This studio is a privilege.

MAE
What am I going to do at a studio?

ROBERT
With that voice? Are you kidding?

MAE shrugs.

                    ROBERT
    Don't you have songs written? Your mother
    says your piano teacher says you're doing
    well with original music. "Prodigious," she
              said. Whatsername.

               MAE [*hotly*]
                  Emily.

                    ROBERT
    Sure. But the songs — your mother says your
         teacher says you've got plenty.

MAE realizes something — then, suddenly
guilty, hides the guilt as quickly as it
appeared.

                    MAE
     Yeah. Plenty. [*Weird throat noise*]
            I can't go in there.

                    ROBERT
                  Why not?

                    MAE
             I don't feel well.

                    ROBERT
    This whole business about not <u>feel</u>ing w —

MAE thrusts open the rear car door and retches into the parking lot. Like a kitten expelling a hairball, she coughs. Then she resumes her sitting position and shuts the door again, quaking a little.

ROBERT produces a bottle of mouthwash from the glove compartment.

                    ROBERT
              Here, take this.

MAE accepts the vial, swigs, swishes, opens the door again, spits out onto the asphalt, and shuts the door.

                     MAE
        Why d'you have mouthwash in here?

                    ROBERT
          Sometimes my client meetings get a
        little... out of hand. [*Raising his finger
      paternalistically*] Whiskey is part and parcel
         for a lawyer, but not a great scent for a
           driver. [*Pauses briefly, gestures toward
          warehouse*] Well, we came all this way.

                     MAE
      Are you kidding? You played me like that, <u>and</u>
      I'm sick, and now you want me to go in there
             and impress some producer?

ROBERT [*blowing past the bits about his dishonesty*] Håvi Håvsstrom isn't just "some producer." He's my dear friend.

MAE
So there's nothing I can do.

ROBERT [*almost withholding a "young lady"*]
That's about right.

MAE hisses under her breath, furious. Together they exit the vehicle, MAE delicately stepping over her own vomit.

CUT TO BLACK

FADE IN on a tidy, pragmatic studio control room. ROBERT and MAE are seated in small, stiff, sensible couches. HÅVI HÅVSSTROM is positioned in the producer's ergonomic chair with his hands latticed behind his head and his legs splayed: the picture of relaxed authority. The man is at least six foot four, and his sharp facial features recall unforgiving geography — a nose cragging like a cliff, a jaw sloping down like a fjord. His long, blond, carefully brushed hair is ponytailed behind his head. He is clad in all white and, for reasons Mae can't fathom, enormous sunglasses. He sports a hefty medallion.

The word "douche" leaps to mind.

The room is exceptionally clean — a pleasant exhale to the rest of the junglelike warehouse Mae has traversed, trailing Robert, to get here. Other than several music industry awards — plaques, certificates, trophies — on display, the only item in here is a well-positioned bowl of candy on the table, probably put there to make artists feel comfortable but which instead comes off as a mildly unsettling attempt to coax or cajole them.

                    HÅVI
        So tell me about yourself, Mae.

          MAE [*avoiding eye contact*]
                I don't know.

          HÅVI [*turning to* ROBERT]
                That voice!

ROBERT, almost imperceptibly, shakes his head.

          HÅVI [*turning back to* MAE]
      Robert says you're quite the songwriter.

        MAE [*still avoiding eye contact*]
                I don't know.

                    HÅVI
        You have some material composed?

MAE [*staring into her lap*]
I mean, if Robert says my mom says Emily says
I do. Then it must be true.

HÅVI
Ups and downs… ah, the artistic mind.

MAE [*snottily*]
Yeah. We're the only people with moods.

HÅVI [*chuckling*]
She doesn't know who I am, with whom I've
worked.

ROBERT [*quickly intercepting*]
No need to get into that now.

HÅVI
One of my clients —

MAE [*finally looking up*]
"Clients." You are both so... clinical.

ROBERT [*trying too hard to be gentle with
her, almost making a show of it for Håvi*]
Mae — Håvi is a very special friend of mine.
Let's give good faith a shot here.

HÅVI
Maybe she speaks not so much through
conversation as through song. Why don't we
sit at the piano? You can show us what you've
been working on.

                    MAE
        I have to go to the bathroom.

Standing up suddenly, MAE runs out of the
studio.

FADE TO BLACK

FADE IN on MAE in a tiny, sterile, private
restroom, prostrate before the toilet,
gasping and dabbing traces from the corners
of her mouth. The top of the toilet tank is
furnished with gaudy music industry magazines
and guides.

She flushes. We hear a KNOCK at the door.

MAE coughs weakly.

                    MAE
                   What?

        ROBERT [*from outside the door*]
                Great news!

                    MAE
                   [...]

                  ROBERT
We're going to move forward with the record!

        MAE [*beyond exasperated*]
        How about a, "Are you alright?"?

                    ROBERT
        I thought it would be in your best interest
                if we told you right away.

                      MAE
        How about asking me first? Or d'you and the
        [redacted] Swede have your own operation
                      going?

Uncomfortable pause.

                    ROBERT
        Mae, Håvi is standing right next to me.

                      MAE
                      So?

                    ROBERT
             So he can hear you.

                      MAE
        Well, he's Swedish, isn't he?

Uncomfortable pause.

                    ROBERT
                Look, Mae, I —

                      MAE
        And he's going to be hearing my voice a lot
        the next few weeks anyway. If I truly have no
        choice but to cut this record. So he may as
                well get used to it.

ROBERT [*almost hungrily*]
So you're in, then.

MAE
It doesn't matter if I'm in, does it? You and
Håvi have already decided we're going through
with it.

HÅVI [*cutting in*]
I've already emailed the session musicians. A
bassist and a keyboardist, both named Alex. A
guitarist, Jonnny Rota, brilliant. Used to be
a little bit famous, actually, almost twenty
years ago now. Robert, I'm sure you know
Jonnny. And this drummer, fantastic. Indian
guy. Don't remember his name.

MAE
You just emailed him, and you don't remember
his name?

HÅVI
It's spelled out in his email address. He was
the business manager when his company helped
me install production software. Help me run
some troublesome plugins. I owe him a favor.
[*Trying too deliberately to pronounce the
name correctly*] A.J., I think. I remember
from his email signature.

MAE
My forehead is killing me.

HÅVI
Come on out and we'll get you a cold
compress. Soda. We have a good care kit for
our clien — for our artists.

MAE
I'd rather stay in here.

ROBERT
We'll get you the best medical attention when
we get home. But first let's show Håvi the
songs you've been working on.

HÅVI [to ROBERT]
Everything on her terms. Just like a past
client of m —

ROBERT
But that voice.

HÅVI
That voice.

ROBERT [to MAE]
You just worry about two things: Creating and
singing. All the money — you don't have to be
concerned with that.

FADE TO BLACK as MAE gets sick again.

Sound dissipates along with the screen, and
we hear chatter fading, too:

HÅVI
Yes, let's talk about money…

February 17th (a Saturday)
Mae

Returning home miserably from my introduction to Håvi Håvsstrom's studio, I've remanded myself to my usual backseat position in the Strand "family" vehicle to face a bad mixture of exhaustion, distraction, seasickness, and guilt. And pressure, of course. And some really crappy ginger ale.

The car is disquietingly quiet. Robert has never had the habit of putting CD's or the radio on, which makes me feel like he's been in the business for the wrong reasons. Shouldn't he take pleasure in listening?

"Håvi is going to email you with some dates," he says, oddly chipper given my physical and mental state. "No reason you can't start next week."

"Next week?" My psychosomatic kitten collar from a few days ago rears its head again to wrap around the base of mine, and my voice now sounds like a strained, unhappy chirp.

"Sure!" Robert says, fixated on the road before us. My questions and responses are afterthoughts to him. "Håvi's referrals are all professional session players. They're not going to need more than a few minutes with each tune to have them ready for recording."

Tune, I think, irritated: everything Robert does feels so anachronistic. As far as I'm concerned, he and Ingrid are still living decades in the past.

"If you've got plenty of songs," Robert continues, "the fun part will be winnowing the setlist down to four or five of your best."

"...or I could decide," I mumble.

"You're right," Robert says, his Kane County Cougars hat bobbing as he nods. "A full album is better. Then you can really dive into the product. You've got the material for it. Really make a statement."

I frown, which Robert can't see — not that he would be paying attention anyway. "I thought this record was just a birthday present for my mom."

For a moment, Robert seems caught off-guard. Then he leverages his composure almost instantly, a trick I assume he's developed from working in a dog-eat-dog field for over thirty years. "Of course," he says. "But that's even more reason to make it really, really good." I think he's trying to look at me now through the rearview, but I can't, or don't want to, meet his eye. "You'd like to make your mother happy, wouldn't you?"

I stare out the window as light snow begins to fall.

"Anyway," Robert goes on, "the result will probably be so good you'll *want* to release it. You'll be proud of it, I think. Håvi is a great producer. Heck — " I can feel him trying to meet my eye again — "you may even get famous."

"I'm going to be sick," I tell him, urgently.

Robert waves this concern away. "It's all this time in transit."

"I'm serious."

"There should be plastic bags back there somewhere."

For all the tidiness of the Strand "family" home — and for as organized as Robert Koenid, Esquire, claims his business runs (or ran) — his personal domain is a mess. All that's back here is that sprawl of CD's from ages gone by.

"Maybe if we talk about something else," I suggest weakly. But we drive the rest of the way to Strand home in silence, and not speaking with Robert allows me to beat the waves of nausea back. Plus, the quiet suits us. There's nothing else to discuss, really.

February 12th (a Monday)
Ajay

Ajay Chadhana is approaching thirty and feels it more with each passing day. Nervously minimizing a window on the dual monitor of the S.P.L.I.T. company-issued computer twice hourly these days, he reads and rereads excerpts from each in a series of studies he's bookmarked investigating unduly high blood pressure in young South Asian men, even the lithe and tightly wound. Chest pain, too, an affliction he's had for most of a decade. If pressed, he could cite dozens of research efforts dropped down from his own menu of links and sub-links on the subject. But no one would ask, and some suffering is best kept private anyway.

In the end, it's easier to blame your genetic makeup, which you cannot change, than your circumstances, which you can.

Driving into S.P.L.I.T. this morning, Ajay wonders whether he's always been so competitive about work. Is it hardwiring? Was it hundreds of sandlot hours of street cricket from childhood through his teenage years? Perhaps those blistering India afternoons primed him for an overextended adult life — a dwindling twenties spread dangerously thin chasing corporate rewards while trying to make it all work as a drummer.

Ajay's life has been a constant exercise in striving and struggling to justify one thing to the other. For the last eight years, he has steadily been climbing the chilly corporate mountain at a project management software firm, sensibly named Systems Planning and Logistics for Information Technology and better known to clients as "S.P.L.I.T." By now, the most enjoyable part of Ajay's career is his commute. The reason? Control. If only for half an hour every Monday through Friday morning, and again each afternoon, and save for every other driver on the road, and notwithstanding the low stakes of his actual authority — temperature regulation: critical; music regulation: essential; the privacy of vehicular enclosure: vivifying — the time, the space, the car, are totally *his*. Plus, Ajay relishes his sharp little crossover's pragmatism, not quite utility, not quite compact. Is it a contradiction to take pride in understatement? No matter: he can tell himself without voicing it: *This is mine.*

Since Ajay's schedule always belongs to someone else, any autonomy is worth claiming for himself — though space, in the end, might be less important than time. One might think a career in project management software implementation and administration would stay hemmed into the weekday hours of 9-5, but it's more like 8-6 if you account for rising early, dressing to assume the part of corporate "solutions leader"-slash-teammate, plus that savory commute. More accurately, Ajay's days tend closer to 7-7 to encompass "workplace prep" early in the mornings and the increasing demand for report review, analytical assignment, or "ideation session" after nightfall.

Then, most evenings after arriving home, Ajay's time is devoted to his second job: a different kind of session entirely. Regimented less in hours than by sprawling audio projects, Ajay's other life as a studio drummer is dictated most often by a producer or engineer — something like the top-down leadership method that constitutes Ajay's preferred workflow for its well-defined hierarchy and organization. Much less favorable, and much more common, is a democracy of amateurs: the group decree of some young, hungry, independent band who will have hired Ajay as a substitute after their own drummer has failed to show, or who has quit, or who has been canned, usually for not caring enough. As a freelancer,

Ajay is thus regularly marshaled for his skill, his flexibility, and a years-honed aptitude: speak softly and carry two sticks.

When not doing session work — or, on especially long nights, after it — Ajay performs in Chicago bars for little pay. The hours, the prep work, the time expenditure, feel like vestiges from his slightly younger days, hairs of the dog and bad workplace practices: you do a certain thing a certain way because you already have. You wonder why, and then you do it again. Still, Ajay has been able to lawyer himself into believing in the professional upsides of this dual life, the tech/punk ouroboros, which he's long given up trying to present to his biological family across an ocean. An underbelly music career has demanded that Ajay:

- develop a mechanically demanding, defensibly cerebral skillset (drums = math, if you feel like spinning it that way), where his contributions make him essential to every working group of which he is a part;
- undergo an experiential method course in relationship-building orders of magnitude beyond what any MBA could possibly teach; and
- reap the perks of the lifestyle:
  - middling acclaim
  - the respect of one's peers
  - the odd pair of drink tickets

Such rewards have become less important and less attractive to Ajay as his late twenties have slid by, especially in comparison with the more hardlined assets a S.P.L.I.T. career offers: his salary, most importantly, alongside a demarcated path for upward mobility — a prospect big with the family, stymied though it may be in real life — and the opportunity for real leadership, crystallized in increasingly directorial roles. To date, these positions have escalated from Associate to Senior Associate to Manager to Senior Manager, above Ajay now only Director and Senior

Director, until the clouds, he presumes, give way to a breathtaking view of the Vice-President-Senior-Vice-President sierra.

For dinner most weekdays, Ajay scarves a hastily assembled sandwich in his car or behind the drum kit in covert gulps between takes. In the backseat of his crossover, he keeps a handful of nondescript tees prerolled in an efficiency-maximizing exercise he has privately dubbed the "freeze-dry method." Thus he can shift, at least in appearance, from the role of Office Guy to the assignment of Careerist Drummer. Given the high pressure on proud but journey-worn "liferism" promulgated by musicians young and old — and, like Ajay, in between — the goal of Ajay's apparel change has never been his *own* acclimatization to the environment; rather, to dispel any impression he might be motivated by a world beyond it. There a little half-circle ensconces him: toms, snare, kick, crash, ride, and hi-hat. Some weeknights, however, don't afford Ajay sufficient time to change, so he materializes on stage slightly more often than he considers ideal in his signature quarter-zip sweatshirt, or, on days with client meetings, a button shirt. At least chinos are invisible from the audience' vantage.

Ajay Chadhana, in sum, is tired. While he goes about everything alone, his exhaustion — the headaches, the endless labor, all bespoke to someone else' needling specifics — unites him silently with a generation defined by its fatigue. He's tired of working in a place that vacuums the soul, that threatens to claim even more of it with cheap promises of title changes, a pool table, free coffee. He's tired of getting up early, of staying up late, of memorizing music, of recapitulating it, just to clear away utility bills for an apartment that's far too small for him to feel at peace. He's tired, especially, of slipping in and out of both roles: project manager by day, drummer by night, each with its own complicated set of social demands, each a self-important closed loop of skills and knowledge, many of them endemic to its own industry. But would anyone call the fragmented ecosystem of music-making an *industry* anymore?

To boot, Ajay can't complain to anyone. Whinging to S.P.L.I.T. management or requesting workflow adjustments would be unthinkable. He can almost hear templatized chortles, perhaps a derisive *squeaky wheel* or *rock the boat*, at the idea. And musician gripes? At thirty, he feels he's heard them all, and often the stories feel like a verbal contest of nightmares — or, worse, are boring. Either way, grumbling to his daytime coworkers or his nighttime musician compatriots is at odds with Ajay's long-cultivated stoicism. More than anything, he's tired of that exact conversation: workplace tribulations. He's sat on the listening side of it two million times, wondering if this is why his family sent him to this country, if this is what it all was for.

Early on this frigid Monday, as on many others, Ajay is meant to report to work early for an increasingly routine 7:45 a.m. "catch-up" with Angela Miller. Though the S.P.L.I.T. team has tried to impose a broad "no messaging on weekends" policy, this guideline, alongside many others on the S.P.L.I.T. life-balance continuum, is often overlooked. Angela, twentyish years Ajay's senior, to whom he and many others report, is known for investing long Saturdays at S.P.L.I.T. headquarters to keep project work churning. Graying, involuntarily austere, Angela communicates so rapidly and concisely her hyperefficient speech patterns can instill discomfort in others, as though her diction is beholden to a company bottom line. Once, on the drive home, the nickname "angina" popped into Ajay's head. But — valuing respect for one's leader, and his own prospects for ascendancy within the company, over a joke contained within his mind — he avoids returning to it.

Angela had written Ajay last night, around 9:30 p.m. on a Sunday, to "ask" that he arrive early Monday morning. Loading out of a gig at local rock club Eddie Momento's at that time, Ajay had been working for Dylan Dee, an aging songwriter who's seldom able to pay Ajay very much but does draw a decent crowd on recurring Tuesdays and, less often, weekend shows. In her phrasing, Angie's crime is not malice but carelessness, which pushes up against Ajay's sensibilities as somehow worse. Subject line: *New client!*

Showing up to S.P.L.I.T. headquarters as requested, Ajay parks, swipes a hard plastic ID at the door, and takes the elevator up one level, where S.P.L.I.T.'s middle management are stationed. The building's overeager conditioning system is already cranking cold air throughout the office. The front desk is still empty, the sun hasn't yet risen, and silent paddocks of cubicles are arranged in a haphazard scatterplot adhering to "modern cognitive workplace design" — quirkily hexagonal computing spaces and "huddle spots" meant to emulate randomness. In disrupting rigidity, in trying to make the S.P.L.I.T. workforce feel more comfortable, this contemporary coddling tightens Ajay's aortas. He'd much rather take and administer orders from the summit down.

Angie, meanwhile, has had her own private office as long as Ajay has worked at S.P.L.I.T. — another cognitive design contradiction that has long yielded a secret envy on his part. Now he adopts a low-rise office chair opposite her faux leather throne. A glass of icewater sweats between them on a slab of plastic which, patterned unconvincingly in the image of marble, is intended as a shared workspace. It functions better as a barrier.

S.P.L.I.T.'s incessant HVAC is running even stronger in here. Ajay shivers.

Angie doesn't look up from the tableau of devices before her. "Good weekend?"

If a tenet of Ajay's dual life is to keep his corporate career separate from his collaborators in music, the repression goes in both directions. The surface level of workplace niceties makes it easier. There's no need to disclose a second income, a second personhood, a second universe of skill sets. Here at S.P.L.I.T., Ajay strictly discloses the tip of the iceberg.

As a very tiny exercise, he tries not responding at all. He wants to see whether Angie notices. He predicts correctly.

Angela gestures to the wall beside her: a floor-to-ceiling dry-erase canvas domineered by S.P.L.I.T.'s value offering in hard pigment in the center. *S.P.L.I.T.*, it proclaims: *Project planning promoting private parties' primary processes, products, profits, people, platforms and propositions.* To its left Angie has scrawled a nimbus announcing: CLIENT: COLDWELL with bullets underneath, each heralding a series of scribbles in her own nearly intractable handwriting.

"I'm going to tell it to you straight, Jay." This hasn't always been Ajay's experience at S.P.L.I.T., but he listens closely anyway. He's also never given Angie permission to truncate his name, but that's never stopped her. "There's going to be a merger," she says as she swirls one cube against another in the glass. "We're going to need you to start working nights and weekends." She pauses. "We're also going to be laying people off."

Ajay's eyes widen.

"Oh, not *you*." This is an afterthought. "But you're going to be a big part of the transition." She cracks a cube between her teeth. "Do it effectively, and you'll move upward as soon as this deal is underway."

Ordinarily Ajay moves quickly, but today he hesitates. He feels that ventricular twinge again.

"We come to work to make money," she continues. "And there'll be more of it after the Coldwell merger."

Apparently sensing his unease, Angie recalibrates in the silence. "Part of leadership is letting things go. People, too." She shuts off the tablet before her by way of dismissal. "I just sent you the proposal. You can read about it at your desk."

Ajay stands up to leave.

"Oh — " Angie adds. "This discussion is *very* internal. No meetings outside our inner circle. And no need to bring it up with the teams in your jurisdiction."

Ajay nods. Mentally he tries to steady his heart rate, but no one, not even he, can control that. He adjusts his backpack and makes for the door. He has more questions, but Angie Miller has turned back to her primary computer, already preoccupied with something else.

February 12<u>th</u> (the same Monday)
Ajay

Most S.P.L.I.T. employees check their personal email after morning meetings, and despite a lifetime of distraction resistance, Ajay often does too. His blood relatives are apt to write him in their evenings; eleven and a half hours ahead of greater Chicago, they ought to be cooking dinner around this time. He refreshes a work messaging portal, prematurely remiss for taking leisure time even though most of his coworkers haven't even clocked in yet. Even then, Ajay imagines he can hear a small contingent in the basement, already enjoying rounds of darts or free caffeine.

He sees one email from an artist named Bryant, the helm of a band called Sensory Overlords, something to do with a gig the week after next, but Ajay puts a pin in the thought for now. Nothing today in his inbox from Mom and Dad — more accurately, Mom, who always signs her digital letters of varying length from both of them, though her particular cross-stitch of condescension and idiosyncratic English shines so personally through her emails it might as well be handwriting.

In whichever back-end personal development cogs Ajay had allowed himself to spin when he'd hit the bed after yesterday's daily sprint, he'd been thinking about his mother's most recent missive: several paragraphs urging him, in language and procedural argument that hardly differed from any of her correspondence prior, to entertain moving "upward and outward" and to find better career prospects outside of SPILT [*sic*] by leveraging his hard skills to secure a superior position elsewhere.

You have been there eight years, the email had explained, unhelpfully, proceeding to ignore the influence and experience Ajay has racked up throughout his last half-decade within the company. He imagines responding with body text pointing to the numerous business journals he peruses almost as often as he does academic research on hypertension, but he won't. And through intention or incident, this most recent last email has also managed to omit any inquiry or expression of interest into Ajay's personal life. Any mention of his music career would be out of scope. No one in Ajay's life seems to know what to ask, or how to ask it.

Ajay closes his personal inbox, which is feeling very impersonal, and commands a S.P.L.I.T. folder to load so he can start his day. Everything in his life is divided in two.

⌒

A nineties kid, Ajay Chadhana spent much of his childhood between wickets on sixty-six feet of concrete pitch in the shadow of a flagship metals manufacturing facility in Jamshedpur, India. There he learned to make the most of an *innings*: one's turn to bat — or, to adopt colonial parlance, their opportunity to possess something desirable.

The largest city in the region of Bihar, Jamshedpur was factioned within India into the new state of Jharkhand in 2000 under the governmental auspice of "bifurcation" — not to be confused with Partition, which uprooted different parts of Ajay's family from the 1940's throughout the 1960's. Ajay's family had moved to Jamshedpur decades before his birth in an effort to put as much distance between themselves and the bigger border. Splits of all kinds: these are the shapes of Ajay's life.

Eight years after the bifurcation of Bihar, Ajay flew one way from Mumbai to O'Hare, neatly folded F-1 visa* tucked under his arm. The plan: study at the secondary level in the United States without breaching the Indian government's stringent interdiction against dual citizenship. Thanks to no small effort by his biological parents, Ajay was situated in Chicago's Little India with a man in his forties, first name Raja, and Raja's son Ira, slightly older than Ajay. Raja was a friend of friends his mother had come to know via pamphlets then exchanged online in the informal Auntie Network of the United States — an acronym swiftly ditched as soon as the more fluid English speakers' teenagers let them know what the letters suggested..

Throughout this second installment of Ajay's upbringing, Raja, awkward and immured by middle age and usually shuttered behind the computer at the vice-presidential level of an I.a.a.S.** platform, was never sure whether and when to play the role of father figure. Raja's own parents had moved from Mumbai to Edison, New Jersey — an entirely different chapter of Little India — in the mid-sixties, several years before Raja was born. Raja's father said it was worth the legal hassle of immigration, and adjusting from ninety-degree India winters to Decembers in Edison, which often dipped below freezing, to pursue a Ph.D. in electrical engineering, which he did, successfully. Raja would sometimes express chagrin at his inability to bridge Little India on Devon Avenue to the broader outcroppings of Chicago to, in his words, "Big India."

---

* **Author's note**: Imagine, if you will, the United States immigration office botching something. In this case, Ajay's enrollment journey to this country was made significantly more confusing by the department's misinterpretation of his first name at the top of the form as an application for the *J-1* visa — an entirely unrelated application for U.S. residency as a foreign exchange student. These people managed to swap two critical syllables not even through ill will but sheer administrative oversight.

** **Author's note**: I.a.a.S here means "Infrastructure-as-a-Service," not to be confused with the Indian and Asian-American Survey, an office within an office (U.S.) that had helped Ajay's family submit his student visa application.

Raja's parents had pressured him endlessly to obtain a Ph.D., too, but he'd insisted this wasn't necessary for a successful career in computer science. He'd been right. In the late eighties, in a gambit intended to showcase his own independence as much as to kickstart his own career, Raja, refusing his father's exhortation, took out all the loans for a Master's degree himself. Things worked out.

One summer afternoon, Raja brought Ajay on a tour of the golf course a few blocks from their home. In a grand gesture he'd rehearsed in his bathroom upstairs, Raja extended an arm outward in overview of the sloping expanse of manicured lawn before them. Of his successful trajectory to wealth and stability, Raja switched code into the cadence of academic Hinglish that had percolated in the kitchen and living room of his own youth.

"Golf..." [he paused for effect] "...is outrageous pastime. No other activity, even in America, compares with its demands for land, water and money." Through sunglasses, he attempted a glance at his adopted son, who was staring outward, politely feigning awe at the yawning escarpments cross-hatching below the pair in two competing shades of green.

Raja pressed on. "I built my own life here. In land of plenty, we made our own way."

⌢

"You nearly gave me a heart attack." This, even after an entire one-on-one meeting with Angela this morning, is Ajay's first time speaking today.

Fred Borman, who holds a menial account management role at S.P.L.I.T. and seldom shows up early, has just appeared at the paddock edge of Ajay's cubicle. Ajay must have lost track of the time, a problem he chalks up to fatigue. Ajay wouldn't describe Fred — department-store button shirts, thinning hair — as close to him, but Fred is probably his most pleasant conversation partner in the S.P.L.I.T. office. Weather and highways: they can talk about these, alongside Fred's various grievances with company leadership. Ever diplomatic, Ajay keeps silent on this latter set, a social cue Fred always manages to miss.

While not exactly a bad influence, Fred has never been flagged as a particularly high card within the S.P.L.I.T. deck either. At best, he's a lower courtier or a nondescript even number shuffled somewhere in the middle. Ajay recalls that Fred worked in human resources (or something like it) at another company for several years prior before growing bored of the paperwork-intensive nature of the old job, opting instead to stumble into S.P.L.I.T. sales, not predicting the ennui in that department would persist about the same, even in the face of complimentary bagels.

At the office, Ajay keeps his hair styled with a neat divide in the middle, a partition that permits his raffish black waves to cascade only after nightfall, when less visual restraint better fits his drummer role. Today, brushing a dark lock out of the way, Ajay asks about Fred's weekend with a well-practiced cordiality. Fred explains he spent most of Friday through Sunday "laying low" by "binging TV" with "the wife." While he walks through some quotidian detail, Ajay's mind and schedule and workflow have slipped under the stress-inducing canopy of this Coldwell merger, and he can't find the bandwidth to listen.

"You busy this morning?" Fred is asking.

"What? Sorry. Yeah. Busy." Constitutionally, Ajay isn't one to apologize, but something about office life often places the word "sorry" on his tongue. Conversely, outside this culture and the pressure he perceives from Angela, Ajay rarely hears "sorry" in the world of rock music. In a place of fierce originality and flouted conventions, egos tend to wax upward — and self-consciousness, in most cases, to wane. Not his, though. By maintaining neutrality, Ajay maintains high ground, a quiet confidence barred only by the physicality of the drums.

"I'm making the rounds to see who wants to play darts downstairs," Fred is saying.

Ajay glances at the ticker in the corner of his first monitor. "Dude, it's barely nine a.m." Not constitutionally one for "dude," Ajay discovered as a teenager the pleasantness of a Hindi accent softening a pair of fraternal "D's," endearing him quickly to the boys in his classes in an over-effort to seem casual. No one noticed. In his present-day world of rock music and software development, the precept hasn't changed. All the boys are older now — technically. None are quite yet men.

"They gave us a board in the lobby," Fred says, "Might as well use it." Before the games begin, Fred has yet to remove his backpack or even to make it to his own part of the S.P.L.I.T. compound. "You can't?"

Ajay recalls Angie's imposition against mentioning the Coldwell merger — even naming it outside this new inner sanctum. "Client calls," he half-lies. "Prepping for a thing this afternoon. Trying to get some actual work done before then."

"Bummer, dude," Fred says. "I'll be in the basement."

Ajay automatically issues a "sounds good," though they both know he won't be joining. He turns back to his computer and realizes he's been holding a tiny pin, wood and metal, in his dominant hand. Ordinarily he keeps the useless little talisman in the console of his crossover. He hasn't consciously thought about it for a long time. He must've stuffed it in his jacket pocket this morning without a thought.

February 13<u>th</u> (a Tuesday)
Ajay

Commuting the next morning while his defroster begins to protest its duties with little hisses, Ajay thinks of Ira, his sort-of-brother, who was entering his senior year of high school when Ajay took up residence in Raja's house at fourteen. Ajay considers how Ira — and Fred, come to think of it; and Angie Miller; and most of the musicians who, like Dylan Dee, hire Ajay to freelance — are older than he is. Maybe this is what makes Ajay so desperate to prove himself. Maybe even more so, to bury that desperation in his heart, throw dirt on top of the hole, and kick snow or sand over the ditch.

In the Indian enclaves of Chicagoland and New Jersey, and in the colonial vestiges of New England up to Rhode Island, cricket enjoyed a slow burn in popularity in the 2000's. Despite the uptick, Ira never cared much for the game, which teenage Ajay — appreciating its elegance and attached to his childhood memories — resented.

Unlike his father, Ira wasn't into golf, either. His only real hobby was playing Seal of Approval® at the arcade owned and run by the Eisberg brothers, a pair of nightlife proprietors and bar operators, a few blocks away from Raja's house. Unless the game had been taken over by another patron, at which point Ajay and Ira would be forced into pinball,

Seal of Approval® was the only activity the pair of sort-of-brothers ever undertook together in the year before Ira decamped to college.

The premise was simple: you, as player one, were a gray seal who had to swim from one patch of ice to another while the sea between them froze behind you, quickening unnaturally with each level. (The game was released in the eighties, when the mainstream American electorate hadn't yet warmed to the idea of climate change. The premise totally worked, though.) After the first level, stakes increased: you also had to defend yourself after human hunters — irascible low-grade henchmen who brandished tiny spears but couldn't swim very well.

After the humans came packs of orcas who dogged you in roving semirandom patterns while you heaved the joystick as hard as you could to get to the other side. Each of these elements was comprised of clusters of pixels in sensible colors, now archaic in their simplicity: black, white, blue, gray, and, if you were lucky or very unlucky, red.

But the objective of Seal of Approval® wasn't strictly survival. You were also meant to collect two sets of items: (1) tiny red hearts that replenished your life expectancy, buffering your health and longevity against cavemen and relentless dolphins; and (2) pearls, for which you had to dive by thrusting the joystick down, increasing your point total when you delivered them to your family of fellow pinnipeds waiting on the ice sheet at the opposite end.

You could depend on the pearls' position at the base of the screen, but they were the harder of the two to retrieve. Hearts, conversely, would appear at intervals as unpredictable as they were fraught with predators. Some popped up at a difficult joystick's tug away, some directly in front of you, and some even behind you, a route most players avoided.

In the three months after Ajay's freshman year of high school, just after he'd moved from India to Chicago, he and Ira formed a purely opportunistic bond by routinely pestering Raja, ensconced in his work-from-home corporate quarters, for permission and for Eisbergs' tokens at the outset of every torpid summer afternoon. Raja would respond, already defeated, by asking whether the sort-of-brothers had done *any*thing productive that day — making use of one of Raja's computer science guidebooks, for example, or engaging in physical exercise. Here Ajay would stare meaningfully at Ira, silently willing him to consider giving cricket a good-faith shot. When that effort inevitably failed, Ajay would volunteer himself, albeit at a diffident tween mumble, for some useful or industrious task. But Ira, invoking both seniority and home-field advantage, would simply extend an entitled hand for chips — which, emblazoned with the Eisberg insignia, looked like gold coins but weren't — until Raja would fish the fortune from his desk drawer and fork them over in a little plastic cup.

Only once, saturated with project work, was Raja in no mood to indulge, and Ira glared so fiercely at Ajay to contribute to the wearing-down of his adoptive father that Ajay had no choice but to take an active role. Heart skipping a beat at the silence, he cited the power of the air conditioning at the Eisberg arcade, explaining with a stammer that he and Ira needed to spend time there to escape Chicago's ruthless summer heat.

Raja cocked an eyebrow. "Didn't you just move here from India?"

After a lengthy pause, Ira resumed distracting his father, engaging in further verbal attrition to win his prize again.* Then the pair returned to the arcade to play Ira's favorite game.

Like plenty of elemental pastimes hauled straight from the eighties into businesses like the Eisbergs', Seal of Approval® had a 2P option that didn't actually allow you to play *with* — more accurately, against — another player simultaneously. Rather, a pair of contestants would take turns, level-à-level, ultimately establishing a winner by point total. Costing fewer tokens, this method was favored by most Eisberg barcade patrons. The victor was determined once all lives were lost.

---

* **Author's note**: In the years that followed, Ira — surprising no one — successfully pursued a pre-law college degree, then a JD. As we speak, he is clambering his way upward to a position as senior partner at a corporate firm in downtown Chicago, putting his aggravating habits to professional use.

Thanks to the experience he'd already cultivated, Ira began that summer as the stronger player, but Ajay's acumen swiftly approached his sort-of-brother's as the sticky months elapsed and melted around them. Ajay made a point of learning quickly. More importantly, he was anxious to bring pearls to the opposite ice cap, even if he was observant enough to know the trophy would take place at the expense of Ira's tenuous pride. Ira knew his way better around Seal of Approval® mechanics, coordinated hand and eye expertly between joystick and display — but Ajay developed the superior strategy. It didn't take him long to figure out that, as long as he dove for the fuzzy off-white squares standing in for pearls right away, you could bypass the human hunters almost entirely, thereby circumventing the need to collect the tiny red hearts that would save your butt every time true physical crisis reared its ugly head.

Ajay's method worked for armed sportsmen and hungry orcas but consistently broke down at level three: the boss: the great white shark. A much more sizable clump of pixels, Seal of Approval's® macropredator moved much more slowly and depleted your full stock of tiny red hearts the second its real estate on the screen overlapped with yours. It was always at this point Ajay's penchant for pearls brought his journey to an end.

This particular afternoon, though, Ajay must've gotten lucky, because his tactic finally paid off. At level three, disregarding Ira's proto-Vegas urging from over his shoulder — "Go! Go! Go!" "Skip the pearls, skip the pearls!" — Ajay lasered his focus down to the minerals on the ocean floor, then back up again, then outward to the finish line.

And for the first time, Ajay made it. He tuned out everything a stranger might have noticed in Ira's voice — a hollering eddy of jealousy, insecurity, exhilaration, anticipation — and hardened his attention on the next level, where a new, smaller cluster of pixels ricocheted at the same pace as the great white on the left side, raring for its turn to hunt. Austere, unfeeling, the machine issued its warning:

"WATCH OUT FOR THE TIGER SHARK."

"It's not even moving that fast," Ira glowered, his mouth inches away from Ajay's ear.

"Shut up," Ajay hissed.

Fourteen-year-old heart thumping, Ajay watched as the boxy primordial numbers ticked: THREE... TWO... ONE...

Then the cluster, the tiger shark, disappeared.

"What the — " Ira started.

"Shut *up*." Ajay threw some serious weight onto the joystick, forcing the lever as far as it would go to the right.

But it was done. Together the pair watched the tiger shark reappear and eat up Ajay's space on the board.

"GAME OVER," the screen pronounced.

Ajay just barely repressed the urge to to meet the atonal, unsentimental thing with violence, to kick it in. Eyes downcast but unable to resist another innings, he was about to turn to Ira in a plea for more tokens when his sort-of-brother breathed, "Oh my god."

Ajay looked up at the screen again, stunned to see a long-time goal take shape: the invitation to enter his name on the high score board. Three spaces for an epithet blinked at him, innocent and unpopulated.

"Technically," Ira said, "we were both playing. So the high score is both of ours."

Ajay stared at him in disbelief.

"I'm older," Ira added.

Ajay's heart raced even harder than before. "You're kidding."

"Plus," Ira continued — had he prepared this argument? expected it? — "My name fits on the scoreboard. Yours doesn't."

Ajay's confusion and ire set in like a brain freeze. Under its slushy surface, he toggled his limited options: he couldn't abide "Jay" — he had only been in the States a few weeks and had already been hearing that error or "correction" everywhere he went — and the first three letters of his name sounded like someone else' identity entirely, an appellate he wouldn't come to know and appreciate until building his career as a session drummer years later.

With what he considered to be admirable restraint, Ajay placed his hand coolly on the joystick. "No," he said. He'd claim his territory with whatever three letters could be made to work. What mattered was that the score was his. Secondarily, and only by a thin margin, was that it wasn't Ira's.

Ira placed his sweaty hand atop Ajay's, a gesture intimate in some other world but perilous here.

"C'mon," Ira said.

For a second time, the nuances of Ira's expression — a domineering plea from Raja's only child, his American-born progeny — didn't have their intended effect on Ajay, falling flat and powerless compared to his own pursuit and his own victory.

"No," Ajay repeated, then lifted his other hand to press the game's only button and adze the preselected "A" flashing before them.

Ira smacked Ajay's other hand out of the way and began to heave right on the joystick while Ajay, feeling he had no other choice, heaved left. Within seconds, the pair heard a sickening metal snap. Like children, the sort-of-brothers glanced around, furtive, wide-eyed, united for a moment against any outsider who may have caught them in the act — but no one had. Then they stared down together at Ajay's hand, which before had exercised some lithe dignity around the knob but was now clenched tightly in a fist around the entire joystick. To their horror, it had separated completely from its mounting plate inside the machine.

Somehow both of Ira's hands were already back in his pockets.

"What are we gonna — " Ajay was starting to say, *tell your dad*, but he broke off: Ira was already shaking his head. There would be no deliberation.

"Technically," Ira said, "it was your hand on the knob."

Even then, Ajay was still prepared to collude, to fight for them as a pair, to shelve his anger for problem-solving's sake, but he didn't get the chance. Before he knew what was happening, Ira bolted out of the Eisbergs' arcade, leaving Ajay standing there alone, guilty, fourteen, clutching a useless piece of metal and plastic.

February 14<u>th</u> (a Wednesday)
Ajay

By now Ajay Chadhana should feel like an ascending member of Angela Miller's royal court, a nobleman currying moderate respect, but he parks in the S.P.L.I.T. lot this morning feeling like a very tired king. He's never put stock in spirits or objects, but the Seal of Approval® joystick has been interred in the console of his crossover as long as he can remember. He and Ira never returned to the Eisbergs' arcade, so no one knows about the little incident, and he wouldn't be able to tell you why he's kept the pin. He didn't mean to hang onto it; it's sort of just stuck around. Today he runs his limber fingers mindlessly over the stem before cutting the engine, slinging his backpack over both shoulders, and crossing the asphalt pitch to the office front door. Days have begun running faster with Ajay's ascension in corporate retinue, and by 8:15 a.m., Angie — or some unknown power-holder above her — has already redacted, in fact reversed, the policy against messaging on nights and weekends. As portended in Ajay's last meeting with her, the company has begun to demand attendance for senior management at some of those junctures. The reasoning: S.P.L.I.T. and Coldwell executives all labor from 9-5 every weekday, and the actual work doesn't stop just because of the merger, so how can the two organizations pull it off without rising stars like Ajay dedicating just two more weekly swaths of their time?

The logic seems perfectly fair when one is actually sitting in Angela's office. There, one smiles and nods. But the same procession of argument becomes difficult to swallow, even demoralizing, as soon as you snap out of it and start to consider your home life.

Given the overlap between this instatement and Dylan Dee's residency at Eddie Momento's, Ajay has no latitude but to bow out on Dylan, and it's imperative that Ajay tell him quickly. Within just a few days, Ajay or Dee will have to recruit someone else for the gig — indefinitely, if Ajay's responsibilities under the new S.P.L.I.T. / Coldwell aegis will continue to grow once it's done.

Having never quit on anyone for anything, Ajay doesn't have an M.O. for amicable departure, but he's always imagined such a thing is better done in person. Ideally he'd explain the immobility of his situation to Dee before or after a rehearsal, but the two of them have been playing together so long they seldom practice for the Momento's residency, which is their only chance to see each other, and Dee tends to be in awfully high spirits on the nights he's able to get onstage.

Dee is such a good guy.

Of course, given the single plane of their relationship, Ajay has no idea what Dee might be doing on a weeknight like this. For now, a text ought to hold his place:

Any chance you can meet up today?

Ajay tacks a "Hey" and a comma onto the front, hoping to soften the request, de-capitalizes the *A* so the edit feels natural, and sends it. With all on his mind, and the already-developed backlog of daily labor, the rest of the workday moves quickly.

Now it's half-past six p.m., and Ajay has finished the sacrosanct drive back to his apartment. As soon as he's tromped up the stairs, un-latched the door, and removed his coat and boots, his phone lights up.

Standing in the entryway, he'd hoped for a response from Dee, but the message is a pop-up from Angie — yet another new breach of S.P.L.I.T.'s fits and starts in promoting work-life balance.

can you come back in for another ideation session

Angela is a longtime corporate leader who has made numerous contributions to the business of technology, so her almost willful lack of fluency in person-to-person messaging never fails to elevate Ajay's blood pressure. Likely she, too, is following orders, or simply making a request of Ajay's time — but her conspicuous lack of a question mark suggests urgency, even gravity, to him.

Or maybe Ajay reads undue pressure in others because it's something he places on himself. Because of the extraordinary strain on him to succeed for having traveled across an ocean to... do what, exactly? Chase the dream of what it means to live in the United States? Whose dream? His mother's? Some elders' in India? And what might the achievement of such a success look like? A title with a corporation, even a higher dollar figure for himself, doesn't feel — in the very back of Ajay's mind — worth the stress. Doesn't justify the bifurcation of his focus, of his being.

An improvement in his living quarters wouldn't hurt, though. In the liminal space of the apartment foyer, Ajay weighs his options: if he tells Angie he can't make it today, he'll probably be exercising his last chance to set such a boundary with her. On the other hand, he knows as a freelancer when it's prudent to demonstrate one's personal commitment to the project by entrenching oneself. Such a move might be a justifiable concession for the larger battle ahead.

Several units away, a dog is barking. Ajay lifts his gaze from the boots he's just removed and casts a weary brown eye over his unit, which, given its size, doesn't take long. Most of the one-bedroom's furniture and all of the dishware have been either bought secondhand via online marketplaces or harvested from the end-of-era grab bags during each of his early-to-mid-twenties leases. Nothing matches the standards of quality one might presume of a software engineer or corporate leader, every item a vestige from the last decade he hasn't had the time or the focus to replace. The television, which he has never had the time or leisure to use, was foisted on him years ago by an old roommate who hadn't minded simply discarding her old one when she (U.S.-born) absconded to some other city to chase her dream. Loitering against the kitchen walls at the edge of the counter are a few pieces of décor once shipped from greater Jamshedpur — a tiny elephant, a ceramic teardrop, a sandalwood office supply case. Ajay has neglected to put them on display. Somehow, though this lease still won't be up for months, the moment always feels too late.

There's no hair straightener or blow dryer on the bathroom counter in Ajay's little kingdom, no candles, no plants, no jewelry, no skincare products, no shoe rack, no pooled couple's collection of records or spices or books, no videogames, no electronic miscellany, no half-finished projects. His entire life, Ajay has never had time for hobbies. Everything he has done gets done.

Across several walls and living spaces, the canine keen is escalat-ing. Sound travels uninhibited in this building — nominally the reason Ajay doesn't practice drums, but in truth, spread increasingly thin at both jobs, Ajay hasn't had time for rudiments in months. He can't parse the purpose of the howl: assertive warning or a frightened defense?

Ajay exhales heavily and takes a brief glance in the gritty hallway mirror, where, now that the sun has set, his reflection has taken on an incidental chiaroscuro under the crummy overhead lights. Manually he straightens his hair, heaves the hardshell backpack back over his shoulder, sends an affirmation to Angie Miller, and puts his boots back on.

"I actually need about forty-five minutes," is Angela's harried greeting when Ajay steps into her office one brisk nighttime commute later. "Things have been getting more hectic by the day. Legal stuff, mostly."

Without looking up from the monitor, she adds: "I'm sure you can find something to do around here until then."

"Plenty of project work I've been pushing out with all these pre-merger meetings," he says, a little too trigger-happy to show initiative. "As far as client-facing — "

"Let's convene once I've looked this over."

Ajay draws his mouth in a flat line. Angie, failing eye contact, doesn't clock his frustration. He exits the room.

Now that the office is desolate and the sky has long gone dark, Ajay feels unsettled inside S.P.L.I.T. headquarters. For a moment he's fourteen again, waiting in the park building near the cricket pitch for Raja to pick him up after the other children of Little India have been brought home. The memory of his dependence on another person, even then, brings on a feeling of vulnerability, which he dislikes. Shaking the sensation, Ajay strides back to his usual workspace and starts to set up both monitors. He's just taken his phone out of his pocket to set it face-down on the desk when he sees he's missed a call from Dee. He glances upward to confirm the door to the stairwell leading up to Angie's office is shut before returning it.

"Hey," says Ajay in a moderate hush.

"Hey, man," says Dee, much more loudly on the other end, over street clamor.

"Okay time for you to talk?"

"Yeah, no, this is great. I'm on my break." Dee coughs. "They give me ten minutes." Ajay hears a sharp inhale/exhale through the phone. He can practically see tobacco exhaust pluming together with frost outside wherever Dee is standing. "What's up?"

"I, um." Ajay rubs his forehead. "Well, I might as well get to it, dude. I can't do the residency anymore."

A pause — lengthier than Ajay had hoped. He hears another inhale/exhale and a hard cough. "Really?"

"Yeah, it's, um. My commitments. Can't be moved."

"Ah... I can't ask Momento's to move the residency. The nights — they need me every weekend here. And every Monday now for all this maintenance and management stuff."

"I know," says Ajay, though he doesn't. S.P.L.I.T.'s indefatigable air conditioning begins to hum just over his head. Shivering, he turns up the volume on his phone.

"They keep the good spots for younger bands anyway. Strictly up-and-coming artists. You know how it is. They'd never give it to me."

Ajay considers saying something reassuring about his friend's age, but he can't bring himself to do it. "I know," he says again.

"Nothing you can do to change your schedule?"

"Factors outside my control." Ajay draws his minimal sweatshirt layers around him and crosses his arms, phone before him on the desk. "You get that."

"Well, yeah." Dee inhales and exhales again. "That's the world we chose. Anyway, money is money. Life is life." Dee knows the scrape. Neither of them would deny the difficulty of what it demands to get by and get on.

There's a pause; eased by time and camaraderie, it's not unpleasant. Ajay lets the quiet hang there.

"You've been doing this gig with me for, what," Dee says.

Ajay sighs. "Three years.""

"Well, I hope I can find someone."

"I can help with that, if you want."

"Maybe." Within a longer pause, Ajay can just make out ashing and disposal from across the line, or at least he imagines so. "Well, I should get back."

"Yeah."

"Yeah."

"Thanks, man, for everything. Sounds like they're, um, keeping you busy over there."

"Yeah." There's a long measure of rest, a sustained final moment of brotherliness, and neither man can read sentimentality over the phone. Ajay, for his part, doesn't try to extract it from within the silence. After pairs of "all right, then," and "good luck, man," Dee hangs up, and Ajay turns back to his S.P.L.I.T. machine, where, in countermotion to his older coworkers' pictures of their spouses and children, the Eisbergs' arcade joystick rests on the cubicle's tiny mantle. He doesn't remember setting it there, but his mind has been spread so thin lately, how would he know?

February 15<u>th</u> (a Thursday)
Ajay

The monitor now displays another internal message from Angie, who's finally summoning Ajay back to her office. He has a feeling it's bad news. Save for the air conditioning blaring overhead, the S.P.L.I.T. office is silent as Ajay crosses the carpet pasture for tonight's meeting. He's left the joystick on his desk, mostly for fear of fidgeting with it during their discussion. To appear distracted would almost be as bad as appearing weak.

"Jay," she says when he enters. He ignores this. Angie isn't looking up from the small mountain of legal-looking documents before her. "Bittersweet update for you."

Ajay feels a hard twitch in his chest. He privately scans the defensible reasons against laying him off — his:

- leadership experience (increasing steadily)
- consistent loyalty (spanning nearly a decade)
- social and managerial distance from the company's profligate darts and pinball addicts (assiduous and consistent)
- impeccable timing

Mentally he omits his attitude of deference, which, around this office, serves as both an inhibitor and a strength.

"Layoffs," she says, finally looking up, confirming his suspicion and inciting a physical pressure against the criss-crosses inside his heart. He resists palming his own chest. "Oh, not you," she adds carelessly. "I need you to cut someone loose. We have a redundancy in sales, and the executives at Coldwell say their organization is already well-represented there. They don't need the personnel."

She says *personnel* like it doesn't mean "people."

"Okay," says Ajay, trying not to sound hesitant.

"Who's our morning bar games guy?"

It takes Ajay a moment to realize Angie isn't being rhetorical. She's thinking of a longtime employee at S.P.L.I.T., but she actually doesn't know.

"Starts with 'F'," she says. "Frank?"

Some vague principle of solidarity keeps Ajay from disclosing right away, but Angie is peering at him intently from her throne across false marble.

He must seem frozen, because she cocks an eyebrow. "Don't you manage these people?"

By way of stalling, he almost says, *I was thinking about something else,* but he can't. So he gives his buddy away.

"Fred."

"Ah," Angie says vaguely. The name means nothing to her. "Well, you have to let him go."

"Okay," he says.

"I'll send you the documentation you'll need."

"Okay," he says.

Angie has turned back to her legal papers by way of dismissal. He stands and heads back downstairs to his cubicle, unsure whether he should pack up, drive home, and get some thinking done, or stay at S.P.L.I.T. and make a performance of overworking. Parked in his office chair for a few minutes, gelid with indecision, he stares at the piece of the joystick from Seal of Approval® and tries to muster resolution in what he must do, as if his opinion has any bearing on the choice. Maybe it's time to head back to the too-small apartment. Like an old man, he heaves his palms against his upper legs as he stands.

"Okay," he says.

⌒

Now it's 7:45 the following morning, and Ajay is once again suspended in his cubicle like a speck of detritus in an ice sheet, trying to decide whether he should bring Fred Borman into a private meeting room immediately upon his friend's entrance into the S.P.L.I.T. office.

Then it happens: "Happy Thursday," Fred says through a yawn as he approaches the partition between Ajay's cubicle and the carpeting around it.

"Is it?" Ajay says, more sharply than he means to. Ordinarily, Fred's blithe hellos are harmless, even a welcome distraction to the stresses of Ajay's managerial life, but today his banality is irritating. Odiously soft, bereft of serious ambition, Fred never experienced the pressure Ajay did growing up. The unforgiving cricket pitch, where it all started: that relentless competition in the shadow of the metals manufacturing facility. The influence of a tiger mother and father whose only shot at success and stability, at least as they saw it, was to pin all their hopes on Ajay. The harrowing student visa application, the trans-Pacific flight to the house of an adolescence under the pall of Ira — spoiled, squishy Ira, who never had to live outside the U.S. or even Chicago, never had to forge his own way; Ira, favored by Raja, whenever Raja had even bothered to pay attention to the sort-of-brothers; Ira, careless, prodigal, now somewhere in the law-school-to-partner pipeline, either making loads of money or climbing a molehill to it; Ira, unpushed, unburdened, un —

"You good?" Even as a perfunctory one, Fred's expression of care is a deviation from his unruffled norm, so Ajay must look exhausted or even angry. Distracted, certainly. Fred is bowling wide, and Ajay can either watch the vermillion cricket ball fly by or take his swing.

"We need to meet one-on-one," Ajay says.

Fred holds back a laugh. His relationship with Ajay is so cordial, so anemic, so casual in its foil to office militarism, that Ajay's coldness and formality come off harsh, too incisive. Then Fred realizes his friend is serious.

"Sure," Fred shrugs. "Over a game of darts?"

Ajay accepts, wishing he had the fortitude not to concede the setting. Originally he'd been planning on marshaling one of the finer private offices near the windows for a few discreet minutes. It's been left dormant for months, a wasteful consequence of that foolish "cognitive workplace design." Before long — presuming the Coldwell merger concludes in Ajay's favor — he'll be claiming that office for himself.

$\frown$

"I'm supposed to lead with the bad news," Ajay informs Fred once the two are downstairs. Ajay has brought with him a manila folder of S.P.L.I.T. protocols for this sort of thing and set it on the counter, just in case. Thankfully, Fred hasn't made his first throw yet; midgame, it'd've been awfully awkward for Ajay to cut in with *you're fired* right when the man was about to take his innings. "What — you've been practicing darts?" Fred grins at his own joke as he picks through a tray of well-worn missiles on the coffee counter.

"No," Ajay says as he waits for Fred to turn around and face him. Finally, slothlike, he does. "You're being let go."

Fred stares at Ajay. "You're not serious."

Ajay nods solemnly.

"You're not," Fred repeats, unbelieving. "Is firing even your thing? Aren't you a project manager?"

"I'm managing a lot of projects right now — and yes, unfortunately, some aspects of organizational restructuring have fallen under that set of responsibilities. This conversa — "

"I used to work in HR," Fred butts in. "I know how this works. You're supposed to review my job performance, my goals, and tell me how I didn't meet them."

Ajay, avoiding eye contact, adjusts the short stack of papers beside him. Having never seen it before, he didn't expect Fred to be upset. To Ajay's sensibilities, Fred's even keel, his permissiveness, are the result of Fred's growing up in a nation where he could take any path he wanted in life (or not) and be unafraid of landing on his feet. Unbidden, Ajay experiences a memory of a cabaret gig some years ago, of hearing a performer introduce a song about unbridled optimism in life choices. Situated behind the kit, Ajay couldn't see the entertainer speaking about the up-down pangs of adulthood and reminding the audience — for the performer assumed the audience already well understood — that you were once encouraged to do anything you wish to pursue, that everyone present had experienced this cossetting since childhood. Where and when did it stop? Though years of practice ultimately steadied his hand, Ajay had become so angry that night he could barely keep time at the beginning of the next number.

Ajay takes respect very seriously, and the prospect of interrupting Fred's staid laziness feels to him like an unsacred thing, a serious boundary to be forded. The sheaf of papers becomes a flimsy physical shield, a two-dimensional podium. "I'm supposed to thank you for your time at the organization, Fred, and connect you with the human resources team so you can get your severance."

"My goals," Fred repeats. Angie's corporate-speak, *redundancy*, skates across Ajay's mind. "Or maybe this termination is more about yours."

Ajay stares blankly.

"Goals," Fred repeats. You don't think there's enough room on the — the hill, the mountain, for everyone to climb. So you feel like you have to push other people off."

Ajay's heart is pounding again. Whether from anxiety about exposing Angie or for inculpating himself or from anger at Fred's obstinacy, he can't attest.

"I thought you were one of us," Fred says.

"What does that even — "

"One of the regular people. The good guys."

It's not about me, Ajay thinks, but of course it is. Either way, he's not going to let Fred drag him underwater as he drowns. "Look, Fred, the organiza — "

"You keep calling S.P.L.I.T. 'the organization'," Fred says, brandishing the useless dart bouquet. "Call it what it is, man."

"Fred," says Ajay, softly. "This isn't a discussion. The decision's already been made."

"You're not even *look*ing at me." Fred slumps finally into one of the basement barstools. "You might as well have broken it off over the phone. Actually, an email would've been just as weird and... and cold as you are." Body still slouching, his eyes begin to dart around, as if reasons to retain him are posted against some wall. "If you were going to fire me — guidance during my time here — ways to improve — can't think of anything I could've done better." Ajay almost pities Fred's blubbering, his imprecision, his unwillingness to take accountability. "But I guess now you can add *severance* to your list of *responsibilities* — "

"I don't have to stand here and provide reasons t — "

"I have two kids."

"Please — " The tireless hum of S.P.L.I.T.'s air conditioning begins again. "Don't interrupt me." Ajay is met with silence, which he supposes is what he asked for. "You also spent most of your afternoons, which are meant to be used for client calls, playing pinball downstairs."

"Darts, mostly."

"Yeah, well. I'm going to need you to give me those, by the way." Ajay motions toward the sprig of three still enclosed in Fred's fist, boastful little S.P.L.I.T. logo emblazoned on each of their tailfeathers.

"Are you serious?"

"Well, you're not going to take them with you." Ajay holds out one expectant palm.

With resignation, Fred unclenches his hand and places all three darts in it. The churn of the HVAC comes to a halt, and the room is still for a moment.

Whatever pride Fred has is set aside now. "There's no way you'll give me one more chance?"

"I'm not in a position t — "

"But as a friend — "

"Don't — " Ajay tucks two of the darts into his shirt pocket, keeping the third in his hand, like a weapon primed — "interrupt me." He motions to the stairwell, and Fred, shaking his head in anger and disbelief, begins to exit. "We'll be in touch with the paperwork."

Ajay remains below ground so he and Fred can return to the main floor separately. Already whirring over his to-do list for the remainder of the day, Ajay unpockets the pair of darts and sets them back in the bin on the counter in their proper place.

After a few minutes have passed, Ajay begins to ascend the steps, still toying absently with the final dart. Out of habit, he didn't realize he's holding it, that he's taken it from the S.P.L.I.T. basement into his own hand. It feels so much like the Seal of Approval® joystick he hadn't noticed the difference.

February 19<u>th</u> (a Monday)
Ajay

Penned in his hexagonal cube at S.P.L.I.T. headquarters, Ajay receives another stilted notification from Angie, accidentally ominous, this one only a rapid-fire subject line:

my office

Without body text, the overtone reads like an assertion or a call from a school principal, but then it occurs to Ajay maybe some accolades are in order after what happened with Fred. Would that be customary? Might it be weird, or perhaps a S.P.L.I.T. standard, for Angie to personally commend Ajay for having fired his low-achieving buddy since the pair of them last conferred in her office? Part of some checklist she has for the Coldwell merger or for Ajay's professional development?

Either way, Ajay has no choice but to head up to that same office now. He blackens the dual monitors before him, a security measure instated to keep meetings with Coldwell higher-ups thoroughly guarded from S.P.L.I.T. commoners. Ajay rises and begins to trek the increasingly well-worn path up the stairs to Angie's office.

By the time he's made it up the stairwell and entered, Ajay has started to imagine he'll hear praise. Even a curt "good job" would be sufficient acknowledgement of the self-sacrifice required to dismiss Fred from the company for good — forever, rather; "good" doesn't seem to be relevant here.

"Jay," Angie says, the icicle tone in her mismoniker snapping him to attention. The stress is getting to him. "I need you fully present for everything we have going on."

Everything going on, he thinks. How very corporate, how distastefully vague.

"You've gained significant trust with me," Angie continues, "and with S.P.L.I.T. leadership above me." Ajay experiences a shiver upon hearing *trust*. By company design, he has never met these high-statured people above Angela. "And there's more in store, if you'd like to maintain your upward trajectory here and throughout and after this merger."

If you'd like to. More pay? Power, even? So foregone it's laughable — why else go to an office job? — but Ajay puts on a little show of earnestness with a nod. He thinks of Angie's axiom: *We come to work to make money.* She presses on:

"We want you to create and deliver a major presentation to Coldwell's executives selling some of the strongest points of S.P.L.I.T.'s inner trappings. The way we conduct our business. If your discussion goes well, it'll be one of the final steps in securing the terms of the merger. We'll be able to announce the happy marriage not long after."

She looks at him pointedly, and Ajay nods again, harder this time.

"Two weeks from now," she says. "Between this moment and then, you'll need to conduct a bulk of internal research on S.P.L.I.T. operations and personnel; on Coldwell's strengths, methods and goals; and on where you think the project management software industry is headed more broadly." He can almost picture Angie's bullet points on her whiteboard.

"That's a lot to cover." He hopes his tone will convey, *I'm pleased with the responsibility, and I'm up for the challenge.*

"You can, can't you?"

"Of — of course."

"Ordinarily we'd have someone help you conduct the research, but I think this effort is best undertaken solo. They want to keep the circle small."

Ajay nods. Angie Miller delves into her private minifridge, a perk of her echelon replete with a personal-size freezer, plucking two large ice cubes before releasing them into her glass of water.

"Naturally, your *regular* work won't stop," she continues. "All the subpoints of your career in project management. Those aren't going anywhere — not now and not after our Coldwell fusion has taken place."

He nods again.

"So that'll be a lot of evenings. More than you're used to. More than you're putting in now. Could be all of them. You'll really need to rock this entire presentation so our blend with Coldwell goes smoothly, and to secure your upward motion here. You can handle that, right?"

Really rock it. Under the cartoon cloud of stress and exhaustion that has formed over his head, Ajay imagines this is the sort of thing American elementary baseball coaches employ to urge their — he almost thinks, *client base*, then remembers those are children. There were, after all, no coaches in street cricket. No coaches in Jamshedpur. Only your competitors and your instincts, just child and ball and bat and wicket against temporary enemy. Your teammates, and your opponents, came and went, shuffled by luck or by schoolyard politics or by whoever happened to be available that afternoon. Concrete and cork and twine and willow and sometimes plastic without a single adult to exhort you to do one thing or another. If that world-within-a-world, across the sea and under a metals factory, primed Ajay's competitive spirit, he wonders whether Angie's flimsy office rally — "really rock it" — is what a young Raja might have heard from golf coaches during his own childhood. Or did Raja develop all those skills himself?

Ajay straightens to rapt attention again when a large chunk of ice cracks between Angela's teeth, then loses it once more when she devotes herself to both computers to retrieve some document or guide that will prime the presentation to come. *Really rock it.* When he was younger, Ajay used to think that would be his job, full-time: to really rock it — to be one of the most versatile, well-honed, disciplined, hirable session drummers this side of Chicago. Certainly to be among the most competitive. That was before more serious ideas about money and about control over his own life came into play.

"Right after this meeting, I'm going to start sending you the files you need," Angie says. "Then you can get to work tonight." She pauses. "I don't see why we can't let you get some of that work done at home."

Let you. More corporate-speak, this time demeaning and misleading. S.P.L.I.T.'s proposed remote work schema seems an awful lot like a self-sanction to intrude into his time and his personal life even more than it already has.

"Thanks," he says. "I already work from home, sometimes, in the evening. Ideation sessions. Report review. Saturdays, sometimes."

He hopes this sounds more like context than griping, but it's unclear whether Angie has heard. "You know what I find helps these extraordinarily long days," she says, veering dangerously closer, he thinks, to inviting private life into their meeting. "One of these." She reaches into her top desk drawer and produces a tiny, colorless, thin, unlabeled pill, apparently within arm's reach, unsecured by any amber bottle, loose in the drawer. "Get the heart pumping a little."

His left ventricle twitches. "Sure," he says, forcing a smile.

"Energy drinks, too. Fine place to start." Angela wrests her own tall can from the fridge and flips the lid, letting the liquid hiss while she drains the last of the icewater before her. Ajay can't read the label, but the font is meant to look frostbitten, caked in snowmelt. Beneath it, a garish animated logo features a blue-and-white mountain. "I'd offer you some," she adds, "but this one's mine." With one index finger, Angie slides the tiny white tablet across the desk barrier. "Feel free to try this one, though. I've got plenty. You look like you could use it."

Then Angie Miller, in her way, turns back to her devices. Having passively accepted her offer, tablet tucked in his breast pocket, Ajay stands to leave, the joints in his legs cracking without his authorization as he does.

February 19th (a Monday)
Emily

Is it really possible to want a life in the arts if you've come from a stable family? Think about it. I'm the only person in the O'Ryan nuclear quartet who's ever taken any serious interest in music, so maybe I'm proof to the contrary. "Everyone likes music" — this was Liam's shrug when I told him as a preteen about my lofty plans for a creative career. He was about to enter college then, already set on a dual degree program in math and physics. Maybe he, classic elder sibling, found my sensitive craft too soft, somehow too nebulous, in contrast to his noble and rigid academics, to take at face value.

Our dad, Dr. Gary O'Ryan, was — is — an astrophysicist. Throughout his own childhood, Dad wanted to study starstuff for a living, so that's what he did. His dissertation fills up the bound blue booklet in his study drawer with *meteor prediction* and *spatial recognition*... and that's about all I can tell you. Physics has never been my thing. Advising over a dozen Ph.D. candidates at a time, my dad often begins his academic lectures by explaining that his area of thought leadership is best conducted in theory. The light years between Illinois and the movements of stars, he'll wink, make it awfully tough to observe firsthand.

If you ran into Dr. Gary O'Ryan in public, you probably wouldn't guess his professional stature as a scientific powerhouse and a curator of rising young minds — a "genius," his colleagues, glowing, would intimate to me at the occasional department dinner party. To you, he'd just be a guy in grubby white tennis shoes and an ill-fitting polo, fumbling for his card in the grocery checkout line or asking my mother Sophie where she'd last seen his keys. Unlike some of his peers, my father doesn't prepend his own name with *Dr.* or *Ph.D.* in everyday life, preferring instead to stick to the simple and unpretentious: Gary. To me, he's simply Dad.

In either case, math and science constituted a pair of subjects so verbally well-worn in our household I grew up thinking our family's shorthand acronym, *emaness*, was its own academic term, proper and mysterious. Throughout my childhood, Dad would regularly bring Liam into his study to enjoin him in lengthy exchanges regarding starstuff and the related topics — a sort of head-to-head in place of heart-to-heart and an endearment between father and child I've always understood better from TV and movies than I have from real life, never having had much interest in *emaness* discourse myself. In most American families, you might picture the men of the family playing catch, watching football, or engaging in something like home auto repair. In the O'Ryan household, male bonding took place just one grade below rocket science.

If there was one advantage in my being excluded from these conversations, it was the opportunity to witness. To understand without speaking — a method I've used plenty in my adult life as an educator. I could capture plenty from my own furtive glances through the glass study doors, where I'd invent mini-trips to sneak by the room at the base of the stairs and conduct little observations of my own. My mother never inquired into my presence, and Dad and Liam never noticed... but I'd imagine excuses for myself anyway, usually that it wasn't warm enough in my room, that I needed to bring up a wool blanket or hot chocolate. To follow, I had explanations premeditated for the already massive pile of blankets by my bed or the heaps of mugs overtaking my desk. But no one ever asked.

The only instances of *emaness* in my own life are the times I got dragged into Dad's study in middle school and high school for having failed some homework assignment or test. I still shudder to envision the dreaded "red slip" indicating less than 50% correct. Hoping to ease my own dread the first time it happened, I tried to break the unpleasant news first to Liam, who shook his head and urged me to share it with Mom and Dad as quickly as possible. While I stood awkwardly behind his desk, Liam pointed at some calculus worksheet of his own to pencil out the analogy: *let the ballast go.*

My dad didn't punish me for my failure or even reprimand me harshly, though, nor did he presume laziness. Not exactly the explosion you'd expect at the end of the *wait-til-your-father-hears-about-this* fuse. Instead, Dr. Gary O'Ryan maintained calm throughout the entire process, accidentally torturing me by walking through every one of my wrong answers, mucked-up equations, forecasts levied way off-base... sometimes in the wrong system of measurement and often by literal orders of magnitude. I don't recall how Dad and I arrived at the right answers, and I certainly don't recall what those answers were, but I recall that he was patient.

Another benefit of my blacksheep status within the family was that my parents allowed me to keep our digital piano in my room. No one else was using it, after all. That's a stark contrast to the heirloom spinets I'd often see in family foyers in my twenties, in the years when I used to make "house calls" (no *Dr.* prefix for me either) as a theory teacher, before Grimm's started handling student enrollment and W-2's and everything else. Those beautiful living room machines are such a great cornerstone for holiday singalongs and family gatherings, even if their placement in the middle of the house tends to be more for parents to keep eyes on their elementary-aged or preteen kids to ensure they were actually practicing — not a necessity in the O'Ryan house.

The luxury of a keyboard in my own room had me associating the intimacy of music with — well, not *privacy*, exactly; more a security that comes with the investment of time and effort you can really only commit when you're working alone. Beyond a positive relationship with

Aurora, my middle school choir director, I did pretty much everything autodidactically. I wish my parents had understood this parallel to *emaness*. Sometimes at dinner, neutrally directed toward Liam, Dad would tell us the most rewarding element of the discipline of starstuff wasn't making major discoveries or breakthroughs or even winning grants or proposals. It was sitting at his desk, solo, halfway through an equation or prediction, mired in science. Savoring the process.

From a young age, I wanted something *more*. More than what — hard to say. But the feeling was always there. Does that make sense? Call it an artistic spirit, a cosmic nudge, perhaps nothing more complicated than work ethic. But once I figured out I had a stellar ear, I wanted to make my mark. To be influential, accredited, somehow. Everyone wants someone to listen. I know I did.

As a child, I imagined I could get so good one day at putting together choiceworthy pop songs I'd eventually bring people into my personal and emotional orbit as an adult. Maybe even fans. Never having gotten another person's ear at home, I wanted my songs to develop a flock of their own. And in my tweens, I spent months of private agony debating how to break this revelatory news — that I wanted to be a career musician — to my mother. Finally adopting Liam's advice about ballast, I confessed it to her in a rare spurt of momentum and confidence...

And she didn't hear me.

I'd walked into the kitchen while she was loading leftovers into the freezer and blurted my big truth, my grand plan. But she wasn't listening. Or maybe she did hear it and decided to ignore it. I'll never know.

After that moment, I waited until Sophie turned back to the counter and saw me — at which point, instead of a maternal greeting or an inviting question about my presence in the room, she just raised her eyebrows at me, as if to say, *Yeah?*

"I, um," I said. "I came down for my sweatshirt."

She turned back to the freezer without a word.

Trudging back up the stairs in silence, I decided then and there I wouldn't be using my talents, my instincts, my ear, to chase noteworthiness for myself. Rather, I'd leverage the acuity in my head and at the piano to connect with people — to help them, and to connect them, in turn, with music, especially if they shared my intuition, my inclination, my interest. To listen to them. And maybe, one day, to assist them in getting the recognition they deserved. If, of course, that's what they wanted.

Desperate for someone to take me seriously in divulging my career plans, I tried the ballast thing with Aurora during our one-on-one voice lesson the following morning: to tell her I wanted a career in music, to use my skills for good. I was terrified Aurora would shoot me down or think I sounded foolhardy or flighty, that my head was too high in the clouds, or worse, that I was trying to derail our lesson. But I'll never forget the way she stared across the piano bench at me, registering my blurt — "I want to be a musician" — with genuine surprise.

"But Emily," she said, "You already are."

Sophie O'Ryan died two years ago. Her life's work was to keep my brothers and my dad herded together, and she was very proud of it. One of the only things she and I shared was a pair of ears for Dad and Liam whenever they needed it. But it wasn't the same between us. She was asked; I never was. She understood their interests; I never did.

But even if my mother didn't care much for music, and even if she didn't take my choices and desires seriously, she had a soft spot for the synthpop that dominated the industry during her own teenage days. As a professional musician now, I have a deep appreciation for the genre's careful production, mechanical finesse, melodic magic, and frequent focus on female stardom. I wish my mom could see its influence in me today.

I've noticed that even people who generally ignore music tend, regardless, to get attached to an artist whose writing and singing voice really speaks to them, even if they don't quite understand why. Maybe you can think of someone like this in your own life. For my mother, to whom I've chosen to extend grace by believing she had earbuds in* the night of my divulgence, I think it was one specific vocalist. In fact, some of my only active positive memories with Sophie are of this artist's CD's playing in her car when she was driving me to school or to a music lesson.

Memory is funny, though: now that I think about it, my mom and I didn't share school commute moments at all. Whatever my age, at whatever time of day, Liam would've been in the car, too, a ridealong that would have tarnished the experience. He wouldn't have enjoyed the genre. Or maybe, deaf to all things outside astrophysics, he didn't even know it existed.

Considering it properly, the only time my mom and I would have been in the car alone together was when she took me to beginner piano lessons. I'd've been seven or eight at the oldest — just enough to register lyrics emotionally and to start to pay attention to song structure. By that point, my ear had me "seeing" the notes moving up and down on the keybed in my mind the way veteran chess players can recapitulate entire games underneath their eyelids. The sparkling patches, the glittering intricacy of synth patterns under pop stars' voices — warm inversions of major seven chords and evocative nines melting around icy, bombastic percussion; arpeggiating fourths and oscillating fifths roaming the expanses of the keyboard. These had my inner vision flickering and bursting like a meteor shower.

---

* **Author's note**: The deluge of science podcasts was just beginning during Emily's preteen years. Her mother kept tabs on these popular rumblings for the sake of maintaining conversation, of encouragement, of motherly facilitation, with the men in her family, especially when Liam would come back home during breaks from college or grad school. That's probably what it was.

My mom wasn't much for singing along to those CD's — she didn't "feel" music that way — but, stealing glances across the console during those brief, rare duo excursions that bumped me up to the passenger side, I could see her mouthing every word. My recollection says I hummed along, but that's probably not true: I spent my entire childhood listening without participating, so why should a car ride auditorily decorated with 1980's singles be any different?

My only vivid remembrance of actually sharing the artist's music with my mom is one night when I must've been nine or ten. My dad had taken Liam with him to a scientific conference, an event that had dominated every dinner conversation for weeks beforehand, to the point where I practically felt like *I* was going. (Is that sympathy or empathy? I can never keep them straight.) Having ventured from my practice room upstairs to fetch hot chocolate on the main floor, I'd recognized the song bleeding from the living room television as soon as I opened the door. I'd only ever heard that woman's voice, those clean, pounding drums, cranked in my mom's car. The sound nearly transported me back into the vehicle parked outside.

Contentedly slumped on the couch, my mom was watching the artist's music videos. Never having seen them, I was blown away. The clothes, the hair, the histrionics, the color palette — they'd been siphoned straight into my eyes from a fantasy, songs I only knew from my mother's dashboard, kindled gloriously into visual life. From the cosmetics to the shooting locations to the neon to the artist's actual mouth taking the shape of each melodic vowel, I was stunned.

I set the mug on the counter without taking my eyes off the TV and sat down, starstruck and silent, next to my mother. Together we watched the remainder of the music video and let the next one play on, both of us transfixed. I recall footage of a tigress or some other large predaceous feline, B-roll of a cemetery or haunted house. But I don't remember that imagery as clearly as I do what happened next.

When the next song began, my mom — *my* mom — got up and started to dance.

For about a minute, I watched her, amazed, not at the quality of her movement but at the fact that it was happening. Then I couldn't help myself: I stood up, too, and joined her. For three or four tracks in a row, we shook our hips as far out as they'd go, nodded our heads in earnest paroxysm, and flailed our limbs in awkward, deliciously unrestrained joy. Not a word was spoken, but a lot was said.

Eventually the tape ended, and we both sat down in separate chairs, panting and sweating. I looked over at my mom, but she was still staring at the inky screen, both our pairs of eyes glazed a little from the reds and yellows and greens that had exploded moments prior in phosphor.

To this day I remain frustrated and a little heartbroken over the fact that I don't even remember the artist's full name. I wish I'd paid attention during the credits, but I was too exhilarated and too young to focus on such details. Still, though, I can picture the artist's face and hear her voice in sharp relief. A few times a year, I'll try and find her music or footage online, but I don't have enough information. As far as I know, her recordings have all but disappeared. If a label or management represented her thirty or forty years ago, I can't find them now. I have the fuzziest memory of my mom saying the artist had made a point of going off the grid late in the eighties, never returning to the limelight, maybe never even fully stepping into it in the first place.

There must be CD's or cassettes or LP's of the artist somewhere, boxed in the attics and basements of synthpop fans of my mom's generation. If I could only remember the artist's full name, I could search for them in online garage sales or vinyl resellers. But the moniker escapes me. It's lost to time. I never asked my mom to spell it out, and now Sophie's gone.

All I remember is the artist's first name:

Ingrid.

February 19th (a Monday)
Jonnny

Time is a candle perched on a toilet tank. How does it come and go as quickly as a matchstick's flame while hardening into memory as lumpy and random as the wax beneath?

Also, a bathroom candle is supposed to mask certain scents. But it doesn't. Not completely.

I wasn't exactly a child star, though it feels that way sometimes. Smack in the middle of two decades at once — my twenties, and the 2000's — I was recruited for my guitar skills by mid-level indie rock band Chyrons. The boys had seen me performing in some battle of the bands in a Chicago basement while they were enjoying a night out, post-show, on tour. Their own rhythm guitarist, they told me, had bailed on their Midwest leg at the last minute because their success had been "moving too fast." It freaked him out. They said as long as I could learn the parts in a few days, I could leave Chicago with them at the end of that weekend. So I did. What else was I going to do with my life?

Chyrons were represented by We Don't Believe in Labels, a label* that housed its own "limber" (i.e., small and crappy) service for record distribution, promotion, ticketing, etc. The payout was never big, and the contracts were too short or too long or too boring for me to read. Still, though, you could actually monetize music in those days. Can you believe that?

---

* **Author's note**: Yeah.

On stickers and in emails, We Don't Believe in Labels' name was stylized as W.D.B.i.L.'s and often known among bands like us as "weedbills." Thanks to W.D.B.i.L.'s connections in booking and tour management, I got to see a great deal more of the continental U.S. in the span of two summer breaks than many Americans see by their retirement, albeit mostly through the bug-streaked rear right pane of W.D.B.i.L.'s' weatherbeaten off-brand passenger van or from the generic plastic furniture outside every lonely highwayside gas station and dollar burger franchise in the Midwest.

In the less-than-fiery years of my life since Chyrons, my memories of that four-year career have long melted into small and unnatural shapes around the knobby stalk of time. The proper fights — creative decisionmaking, differences in relationships with our middling fame, competing personal interests, and the ugly scaffold of money — were already starting to congeal by the time I was twenty-nine. But it's taken longer for me to let resentment fade when it comes to the little things: sleeping arrangements, logistics, responses to gear theft, and a distressing increase in the need for my bathroom stops with each passing year.

Chryons put out two perfectly fine records in the late 2000's and quietly disappeared. At the time, our songs were praised for their "projected staying power" and commended by journalists and tastemakers for "folding the past into the present — collapsing," as one *Retrospector* reviewer put it, "the best elements of classic rock's golden age into the innovative production and self-aware lyricism of indie rock's heyday." I never paid attention to the words, credited to Chyrons' primary songwriter Dave Starkey, but if the pundits boosted my short vocation as a rock star, I was all for it. Most importantly for our "career trajectory," Chyrons fit the "profile" W.D.B.i.L.'s management had identified for "growth."

Then the profile changed. When weedbills leadership cut us loose for "commercial reasons," something to do with "industry shifts" way above our heads, Chyrons finished our two-album contract, emptied about half of the cardboard boxes of our second LP, *If Bedlam Stirs*, on tour, and dispersed across the country like smoke after a fireworks show. I haven't kept up with the others since then. I understand Dave, whose ego I couldn't stand by the end of the Chyrons trail, is a record shop owner on some outer moon of the indie rock universe — a little storefront, I think, somewhere on the East Coast. Chris has married into decent money and now engineers DIY projects as a hobby. I don't even remember his last name. See how even the important things slip away? "Other Dave" is selling cars, or fixing them, or something.

Me? I live, if you can call it that, in a matchbox in the city. I pay part of my rent with the royalties that still drift in through the mail, leftovers from my Chyrons days. Those envelopes are so thin, their contents so meager, you can literally see through them. The entire W.D.B.i.L.'s organization has long fallen by the wayside — "you've probably never heard of it," a *Retrospector* critic might sniff today — but the PRO's and collections organizations still hang around. Lawyers and spiders crawl out of whatever woodwork to trawl the Internet for old CD and vinyl resales and, more recently, occasional streams from nostalgic fans. I don't keep up with the specifics, which are complicated and annoying. They're indecipherable by design. The attorneys belong to no one. The music belongs to no one. The money belongs to no one. But the financial injection, however small, doesn't hurt.

I also pick up the occasional shift at Stoked, a record*keep*ing shop (not to be confused with a record sales shop) of questionable legality. Run by digital music archivist Miles Emery, it's basically a big old virtual vault containing CD's — strictly from the 2000's — that Miles has burned of his own accord. Emery's mission, he's proudly told me, is to preserve pop and rock albums in one place for posterity, even when fans and industry personnel have long forgotten about the original release. He has a soft spot for the aughts. The hours aren't good, nor is the pay, but it's mindless, and I like that.

I supplement the remainder of my expenses with session work from old contacts or from people like Håvi Håvsstrom. Usually the call will come from a touring buddy from the zero-zeros, or, once in a while, an old supporter — a relic of Chryons' glory days who's somehow unearthed me online. They're post-post-punks now, holding office jobs, happy to cash me out much more handsomely than any weedbills "executive" ever did. I almost never report physically to a studio, instead waiting til the afternoon of the session to learn parts by ear, scribble a few cues for myself on the back of a takeaway bag or receipt, track it at home, and fly the whole thing out digitally. I spend most of my time dissolving into my crummy couch, conveniently not far from the toilet.

I'm not totally done with the business of music, but it's awfully painful to scrape the sky of success that young and then fall back to Earth so quickly. Most days — irritable, lethargic, extinguished, deflated — I feel like a ghost in this crappy apartment. Some middle-aged heads talk about the 2000's like it was the peak of music and culture, the same way Boomers talk about the seventies, like the American recordmaking business was the most important empire in history. The overtone is that the inspiration for all the good stuff those days — pop, garage rock, pop-punk, hip-hop, indie — has come and gone. *If that's true*, I'll think, *then stop complaining and make something worthwhile now*. But what am *I* doing?

So an old fuse reignited in my brain when Håvi Håvsstrom emailed me a few nights ago to invite me to work on a record with some young singer named Mae. The sessions start tomorrow, I think. Håvi framed the whole thing as a pet project, which is ideal for me; there's no association with fame or influence. At this point in my life, I've given up entirely on both. (*But you're only in, what, your early forties*, you might argue. And to that I say: *whatever*.) The element that got me invested is Håvi's repertoire. The guy has worked across every genre, and he's been active since the early eighties. He and I have worked together once or twice, but only remotely. The inspiration for his occasional calls, including this one, is my history with Chyrons, which few remember. In other words, my only real proximity to Håvi Håvsstrom is in the positioning of our names in the liner notes from one or two CD's across the years. But my name is always printed much smaller than Håvi's, and no one reads those anyway.

February 20th (a Tuesday)
Jonnny

Late this morning, I arrive in my battered jalopy at the address Håvi Håvsstrom provided for the studio. His email said he'd leave the warehouse front door unlocked for me, which turns out not to be true, so I try calling him when I get there. I've predicted, correctly, that there's not much service down in the control room. The phone goes straight to voicemail twice.

I'm early. My car clock is always off, but I can never remember whether it's ahead or behind, which makes transit a pain in the ass. I have no choice now but to either stand outside in the cold or to load all my equipment back into the trunk, which feels like penance for making good time. Also, my stomach hurts.

A trim little crossover pulls up — efficient, sensible, and, according to my phone, perfectly punctual. The engine shuts off, and a slender desi-looking guy exits the vehicle and nods at me. His thick black hair is willfully unkempt, the way I keep mine, but he's dressed in much nicer clothes than mine. Half-opening the car door, he pops a cymbal bag out of the backseat and heaves it over both shoulders.

"Ajay," he says by way of introduction. "Like 'a J,' but just one of them." I think he thinks I recognize him, but I don't. With a light accent and a consistent rhythm, he qualifies: "Genuine Failures, Eddie Momento's, a few other spots."

Is he giving me his résumé?

Why are we like this?

"You play out often?" I ask, sliding into the same social convention. He nods. "Overworked." Obviously stoic, he doesn't seem like a complainer; the claim strikes me as a reflex. While he talks, I remember instantly how much I can't stand the way so many of us instrumentalists speak to one another — singularly focused on our careers, old guys (it's always *guys* that behave like this) trying to act younger, young guys trying to act older, *tell*ing our compatriots how great we are instead of waiting for the chance to show it. It's rare to find a player who possesses more incendiary instincts — someone who opts to stay quiet until their opportunity to shine. I wonder which of these archetypes fits Ajay. As he continues, I can almost feel his repression, like he's been dividing parts of his life and locking them in his chest cryogenically. He moves quickly, speaks efficiently, and accents his list of achievements with big eyebrows' little motions, all while maintaining complete self-control. His diction keeps me at a respectful but semiformal distance. The pace is downright businesslike. And if he's cold or uncomfortable out here, he doesn't show it.

I haven't spent much time around people in the last several years, though. I might be reading into it too much.

I have to go to the bathroom.

"You?" he asks.

"I keep to myself, mostly." Ajay hasn't asked me my name, which is fine. If he does, I'm obligated to punctuate it with "Chyrons — if you remember them," or something like that. My calling card is tucked firmly in the past, and there's nothing I can do to change that.

I don't get the chance, though, because Håvi Håvsstrom has just heaved the warehouse door open. Now in his forties or fifties, clad entirely in white, he's sporting enormous sunglasses and leaning on the threshold with the weight of a six-five Scandinavian. I'd recognize this powerhouse anywhere.

Håvi nods at me, shakes Ajay's hand, and ushers us calmly inside, not offering to help me with my gear, nor I with Ajay's. Without speaking, I haul my crap down a mechanically cluttered, poorly lit hallway. Ajay follows Håvi's lead while I bring up the rear. We're surrounded by bolted doors, metal lattice, and loose copper piping. I half-expect to see animal movement on the warehouse floor.

"We're here," Håvi Håvsstrom says.

Urgency increasing, I aim for a "Mind if I use your restroom" or something daddish about a pit stop, but all that comes out is a rushed, guttural "bathroom."

"No one else is here yet," Håvi informs us. "That singer, Mae, says she's running late. Train's not on time." He shrugs. "Factors outside her control."

A wet gurgle passes through the middle of me so assertively I'm afraid Håvi and Ajay can hear it, and for a moment, Håvi Håvsstrom's supermassive influence, his catalogue and versatility, don't matter to me. Only my body is setting priorities. Finally, the Swede, moving much more slowly than I'd like, unlocks the studio door. As soon as it's open, I shoulder past him and make for the toilet as fast as I can.

⌒

I can handle pains of the mind — I've been dealing with those for decades — but lately it's this business of having a body I can't stand. Two hours now we've been sitting in Håvi's studio, still no word from this singer Mae, and I've used the restroom three times. Currently making good on my fourth visit, I'm flipping through Håvi's phony curated reading list, whose placement on the toilet tank feels perfect. The one on the top is *Songwriting for Beginners* by some hack I've never heard of, who's very proud of his Ph.D. in Musicology and some string of hitmaking in the seventies that does not interest me. It's not even worth opening. It takes me half my session in here just to get through his name: "Dr." Stuart Hudson Jackson-Margolis. The contents look awful, disposable, fake.

You can tell from the artwork. Call me judgmental, but it's true. Plus, I think self-help — alongside self-care, and self-love, and self-promotion — is useless.

I flip to the next publication: *Turn Your Songs Into Brands, Your Brand Into Fans, and Your Fans Into Sales!* The jacket alone makes me want to vomit. At least I'm in the right room for that.

I strain to hear any conversation between Håvi and Ajay. I'd like to better understand this elusive drummer — especially if, as albums tend to demand, we'll be spending hours stuck together in small rooms. Trailing behind them during our walk down here, I half-heard Håvi thanking Ajay for some contribution Ajay had made to the studio. Production software or something. It sounded like a big project. Maybe Håvi hired Ajay on this Mae album to return the favor.

Something disheartening leaps to mind. I wonder whether Håvi brought me onto this recording effort as... charity. Doling out graces of this kind — it seems almost like a game to people in power, especially if they have a flair for the scattershot. *Sure, invite Jonnny. Why not.* But still, Håvi always said he was fond of Chyrons, and he told me he enjoyed my guitar work. He probably intuited my *situation* (a word people use to dance around money, which I hate; at least Håvi didn't) the last time he and I video called about tracking instruments remotely. The view from the old laptop camera would have given away the inside of my apartment, therefore my quality of life. A lot of musicians maintain a carefully haggard appearance, but I must've appeared truly broke. Broken.

Plus, though Håvi has worked across genres, I'm pretty sure his specialty is synthpop. It's in the man's blood. With less use for guitars and drums in that department, his call list for rock instrumentalists is probably shorter and less essential — so this time, he reached out to a has-been like me and (if Ajay is a software specialist) a sort of partial player for percussion. Who can guess? I'm too proud to ask, and I'm not going to be able to read it through Håvi's massive sunglasses.

But right now there's nothing audible. All three of us are men of few words. Håvi has to defend his authority and a little mystique, while Ajay comes across so tightly wound it's hard to imagine him offering up more than a few little trash-compactor cubes of "yes" and "of course" and maybe sometimes "no." But I could be overinterpreting. For my part, I already said everything I have to say, back in the 2000's.

But Ajay is visibly ticked upon my reëntry to the control room — not at me, I assume, but at the situation and probably at this singer Mae. He's holding a few fingers to his chest, then wrist, like he's trying to monitor his pulse. He interpolates these little check-ins with sips from a tall blue-and-white can that looks and smells like an energy drink. He also fished a little white pill from his breast pocket and swallowed it, probably thinking I didn't notice. Maybe it's for a headache. Maybe not. Looking at the can, I think of my own checkered past with stimulants and shudder. On a Chyrons tour twelve or fourteen years ago, I'd've slammed its contents in a few gulps — and definitely tried that mystery medicine — but Ajay is taking minute, measured nips, like he's premeditated the intake of guarana and caffeine and aquamarine-number-five or whatever to pace with today's preproduction and drum tracking. And now, being more than two hours late, vocalist Mae has messed up all of Ajay's perfect timing.

Håvi Håvsstrom's hands are laced behind his head, legs stretched in a big triangle. He doesn't seem to have the compulsion to kill time on his phone. Apart from his brief breaks, stepping outside once to confer with the entertainment lawyer who brokered today's session, I wouldn't have even thought Håvi owned one. The only sound in here is the gentle whir of Håvi's triple monitor behind him.

"Traditions," he says lazily, breaking the lull. "You have them?"

We're both a little startled; I've only just sat back down, and Ajay is thoroughly sucked into some document on his phone.

"Before a big show," Håvi qualifies. "Or on the road. A lot of musicians, a lot of athletes, have them. Superstitious."

I shrug. "Always hit the bathroom before you leave."

Håvi gives me the elder statesman's look of recognition: *You're younger than I am, but you're right, and I know what you're saying even better than you do.* He turns to Ajay. "You?"

Ajay has trouble unpeeling himself from his phone. "Tiny piece of wood. I keep it in my car. I'm not really sure why."

"Like a drum stick," Håvi says. "Is it for good luck?"

There's a half-pause before Ajay glances up from his device, but he doesn't respond. He may not have understood Håvi was posing a question. Then his eyes move back down again.

"You have it today?"

Without looking away from his emails, Ajay trawls one-handed in his coat and pants pockets, turning up nothing. "Not on me."

"Still wearing your jacket," Håvi observes.

"I'm cold."

After another quiet few minutes, Håvi's phone goes off a third time. He raises a finger: *hush*, as though we needed it. He stands up and exits the room, and we hear him tromp up the grated stairs outside the control room to the ground floor.

Now the space is silent again, infused with that weird partial tension as Ajay remains immersed in his device. I don't have much to do on my own phone. I've never used social media or other feeds, I keep very few personal contacts, and I don't read or watch the news.

I feel a depression coming on. It moves through me quickly. Everything does.

I survey our surroundings to try and alleviate my own boredom. Håvsstrom's control room is exceptionally neat. The place is almost completely clear of cables or even musical instruments, anathema to the jungle outside. The only equipment in this room is the sleek triple screen, which blinks placidly with some past or present session, and a preamp tucked calmly into a pragmatic cabinet.

There's also a practical little coffee table, probably made of the same faux material as the case and thankfully devoid of the "industry reading" meant to help Håvi's clients kill private time. The only item on it is a bowl of untouched candy, which seems to've been positioned there to make clients feel welcome. I grab a few jelly beans and pop them in my mouth, chewing quickly and relishing the sizzle of sucrose on my tongue. It occurs to me that offering this cheap sugar rush — easy, inexpensive and insipid — is the sort of practice those crappy business books advise. I get depressed again. I rue the falseness.

Other than the couches Ajay and I inhabit at opposite ends of the room, the only other thing in here is a small, ancient-looking television. The actual "set" looks very 1980's, which I recognize only from zero-zero's movies that pay homage to the glossy decade. I can just make out what looks to be some rerun, maybe a highlight reel, of a baseball game from around the same time the TV must've been manufactured. Even through the grain of the old thing, you can tell from the uniforms and color palette. The whir of Håvi's computer temporarily expires while the quality and signal of the old broadcast fuzzes up and down. I discern an announcer whose inflection sounds 1980's, too. He's commenting on some player who was supposed to be at the top of his game but has just struck out: "...he was a real firecracker, that one..."

I can't help wanting to enjoin Ajay somehow. In my Chryons days, our default was to piss time away with little games on the road — observational humor, spotting license plates, judging the junk in other people's cars. More and more near the end, the others, tittering, started to clock the miles covered between my requests for a bathroom break, inching toward smaller and smaller figures as the short years wore on. I think some bandmembers' weedbills bills even changed hands over it.

"Hey," I hiss playfully across the control room, pointing at the little screen. Thinking of no other qualifier, I add, "baseball."

Ajay grimaces, still not devoting any focus outside his emails.

"Not a fan?"

"Never been interested."

This is my not-unfriendly tone, developed for competitive men passing time in the company of other competitive men. "Oh, yeah?"

Ajay sighs and mumbles something about cricket, about how people want to compare the two games despite the fact that they're nothing alike. There's a note about Britain in there, but I can't quite make it out.

I employ the same tone: "You don't say."

He shrugs. "No one in my household played baseball anyway." A little snidely, he adds, "We were a *golf* family."

"Oh, yeah?"

"Everyone in the family was competitive. But each of us only wanted to compete with ourselves."

I start to get depressed again.

There's a rattle of keys outside the door, and Håvi Håvsstrom reënters the control room.

"Gentlemen," he says. "Mae had to transfer trains. Now she's stuck on one. She's going to be another hour."

"Another *hour*?" Ajay says. "No offense, but I can't do that."

"None taken, but the session's been booked. I have to charge Robert for it."

For the first time, Ajay makes eye contact with me, and we share an immediate understanding. I don't know who Robert is, but I know, soundlessly, what Ajay means..

"That lawyer's paying for *our* time, though, right?" I say. "Mae's dad?"

"That lawyer?" Håvi repeats with a laugh, giving me a look of surprise. "He's not M — well, yes, he's paying for it."

"Then you two can work it out," Ajay says, pulling his coat more tightly around himself. "I have to go."

"Your drums are already set up," I venture. Money-wise, I need these hours, and I'm very understimulated with work. For me, it's well worth this farting around. "It'll take another fifteen minutes to break them down."

"I already missed work for this," Ajay says, sharply. "What's done is done."

No, it isn't, I think: what's done is never really done but is always rocketing through us still, or at least it feels that way to me.

Håvi shrugs. "I get paid for the session either way."

Ajay and I meet eyes again. "And so do we," he says. He looks at me in silent acknowledgement. If money is the only thing bonding the pair of us, I can live with that. And these days I'll take acknowledgement when I can get it.

Håvi sighs, less interested in this part. "Yes, and so do you."

Ajay rises. "I'm going to tear down quickly so I can get back to work." He exits the control room and descends the next set of stairs to the drum booth so he can disassemble the kit. He doesn't ask for help, and we don't offer it.

February 18<u>th</u> (a Sunday)
Mae

My mother is a ghost.

Floaty, draped in white, stuck in the interior of the house like she's part of the building: textbook phantom behavior. Ingrid isn't scary, exactly, but for her to put so much pressure on me while she is so indistinct — the idea gives me chills.

Every ghost had a past, a life, a different state than the one they occupy now. Something that came before. And if they have one reason for hanging around here, one quality that defines them, it's unfinished business.

Maybe Ingrid's unfinished business is me.

February 20<u>th</u> (a Tuesday)
Mae

I lie in a lot of places, but my bed is my favorite. It's an even better place to drift mentally than my commute to school, which will happen in a few hours. Procrastinating that official start to the day, and wondering why Ingrid hasn't yet come upstairs to wake me, I've been doing what I do in place of taking action on anything: ruminating. This morning's subject is that nauseating record producer. *Håvi Håvsstrom*. The way his eyes practically filled with dollar signs (or Euros? krona? whatever), when he heard me speak. "That voice" — that's what he'd said to Robert a few nights ago. Håvi looked almost hungry, the way Robert did after I was forced to speak up in class in September. Why did he put me up to this?

Eventually I force myself out of bed and begin to head down to the living room, brainstorming confrontations as I approach the stairs. Robert will be at work by now, so Ingrid will have to suffice, even if she's not the source of this problem. Impulsive, but what else am I going to do?

With Ingrid, all my contenders would start with, "You never told me," followed by... something. But what? I don't know *what* my mother never told me, which makes it impossible to ask. I'm hoping I can fire off my suspicions in Ingrid's direction with just the right mixture of aggravation and vagueness to provoke a confession from her. Convince her I already know more than I do. Invert a parent-child *gotcha* when it comes to truth-telling.

But depression's grip on Ingrid today isn't timing out very conveniently for the ambush I'd been planning. When I enter the den to the sound of her gentle breathing, her failure to come upstairs to rustle me is self-evident in her body, which is curled in a logarithmic spiral on the couch. Catatonic, bundled in terrycloth, she's facing a television flickering with old advertisements so irrelevant to anything, the volume so quiet, her attention to it, if she's even awake, could only be passive. That's what Ingrid is: passive. And by pushing me for so long to pursue music seriously, and now to make this album with Håvi Håvsstrom — by deciding what's important for me and forcing me to act on it — she's made me passive, too.

"Hey," I say softly from behind the couch. At my greeting, both her eyelids open halfway, lazily, like a housecat interrupted from a dormant afternoon.

She doesn't respond, but I'm accustomed to living under Ingrid's shadow, her lethargy. But maybe there's more to Ingrid's low spirits than that. She must have been more energetic than this once. More curious, at least. Livelier. I wonder what she wanted for herself when she was my age. What she'd envisioned for her future. I'd like to believe she craved more than this life: dozing in front of the TV, pushing a moody daughter in and out of the house for vocal lessons, letting an entertainment lawyer court her and hang around. Did something once wreck Ingrid's pride?

Or has she always been like this? Depression seems core to Ingrid's being, at least as long as I've been aware of things. Plus, made in her image, I'm awfully meek, too. Maybe Ingrid was just as lost at age twenty as I've been feeling my whole life.

Or maybe it all compounded. Hunkering in this house for so many years, nesting herself as far as possible from other people, hiding from whatever's in her past — that couldn't be good for anyone's mental health or self-esteem.

In either case, acclimatized to my mother's silence, I don't take her current behavior, or lack of it, personally. She's probably languishing this morning just because that's what she does, who she is. I can't confront her now — not because it wouldn't do me any good, but because it just might finish the process of breaking her heart.

Drifting into the kitchen for milk and coffee, I'm beset with an image, hopefully years from now, of Ingrid on her deathbed, finally coming clean. In her last moments, she'd be compelled to tell me the truth about the cogs of her prior life, whatever they are, and how she's nearly disappeared. However these ultimate explanations might turn out, wherever they might fall compared to my imagination, I'll derive a tragic satisfaction in nodding solemnly at this last disclosure and whispering something like, "I've known for a long time."

Until then, I won't have a choice but to stomach my mother's sadness and its nasty habit of seeping into everything around her — a stomaching that includes finishing this album with Håvi. By now, Ingrid must understand that I'm not personally invested in music as a professional pursuit, though (or maybe because) my love for music is best conducted in private. I wish she understood how complicated it all is for me. I wish she understood how much I enjoy singing, how much it means to me. But my whole life, I've only been working at music for her.

A little noise from her surprises me, but it's just a yawn.

"You have school today?" she says.

"Just a lesson with Emily in a few hours," I call back. "I'm gonna hang around here and get prepared for it."

"That's my girl."

Again, I consider the accusations I've imagined throwing in my mother's direction. But those are a problem for the future. I don't know when. The more I think about it, the more painful the very idea of being in the same room with Ingrid becomes, and I turn around and scamper back up the stairs to my bedroom, leaving my hot coffee and cold milk on the counter and my mother still on the sofa, saddled with pillows, half-asleep.

February 20th (a Tuesday)
Mae

The train ride to Grimm's Academy is long, but I don't mind. If I owned a car, I'd pass the time singing for myself. Usually behind on schoolwork, though, I tend to spend most of it cramming readings, or, ignoring those, staring out the passenger window at the fleeting cityscape/roadside combo and doing what my mother calls "getting some thinking done." This sort of aimlessness, a vacancy, is something she and I have always shared. She or Robert or even Emily might picture me using the train ride to scribble lyrics or chords into a journal or other devoted place. But in reality, the very idea of school sucks away all my creative impulses. I much prefer to drift. My destination is grim, but the act of getting there isn't so bad.

Here's why I hate school. I can't stand structure when it's used to constrain us. I can't stand when someone explains something I'd much rather *feel*, and I especially find so much of the goal orientation — an 'A' or a promotion or a gold star — inauthentic. It's cold, and it's not really tied to reality. But Ingrid has always insisted that I show up at Grimm's because she never had the chance to go to college. She could go back to school anytime she wants, but her blank stare isn't worth the argument. Since near the beginning of this school year, the day Robert pulled me aside to compliment and use my voice, he's worked out some kind of financial arrangement with Ingrid to ease the burden of my education. That's what it is to me: a burden.

Aware of the train ride's recurring hour-between-places, Ingrid often plies me with album recommendations to study. Many were released in what Robert calls *the halcyon seventies*, but even more date to the decade afterward, when Ingrid just happened to be coming of age. Older music fans love to ascribe special greatness to their own teenage favorites, trying to turn their own nostalgia and personal taste into something objective or universal. Basically none of Ingrid and Robert's suggestions derive from the nineties or the two-thousands (which Ingrid, appropriate for her dismissiveness and depressiveness, calls "the zero-zeros"). So that's a gap of twenty years. Then a dependable chunk will have been released in the most recent year or two. I always wonder how Robert and Ingrid find them. I suppose Robert keeps up with the producers and industry personnel — people like Håvi — responsible for pushing these albums out. But for Ingrid's part, I can't say.

Having no problem lying to my mother, I typically wait until the train ride back home to stream the two or three most popular tracks, or just snippets, from whichever album Ingrid and Robert have most recently pushed on me. Then I skim its Canonymous* page for reviews and Ingridworthy tidbits with the efficiency of a kitten monitoring a brick wall. This way I'm ready to arrive home and regurgitate the passages I've poached from press to my mother. She's never the wiser on my un-thorough listening. Robert, thankfully, is often still out with clients when I return from class. Semi-retired.

On this particular morning I let my thinking-stare toggle between the grubby train window and everything racing past it, and the blank pages of a notebook where I'm supposed to've written down three things I saw or did this week that could be made into song concepts. Does that task sound tacky, boring, or excruciating to you? Now you better understand my problem with school.

---

* **Author's note**: Published and edited eusocially online, freely available, and putatively all-encompassing, Canonymous has long hailed itself as "the entertainment scholar's most official unofficial encyclopedia" of "everything important in art and media." [*Rhyme unintentional.*]

Today's instructor, Prof. Stuart Hudson Jackson "The Jackal" Margolis, is some washed-up pop writer who, much like Robert, is "semi-retired." He never misses an opportunity to remind our class he's spent decades contributing to hits out of Los Angeles, none of which have been released in the last thirty years, and none of which I've ever heard, or heard *of*, though H-J-M clearly expects everyone in the class to've explored and enjoyed them. I suspect he knows Robert from both of their glory days, which I assume in turn is how part of my Grimm's tuition gets paid. It's all over my head.

In his exhausting lectures, the Jackal is constantly citing his "personally curated pantheon of historic songsmiths" who made their mark on culture by "shapeshifting any headline, emotion or quotidian observation" and setting it to melody in a "tidy, elegant, three-minute pop construction" — something with "real staying power." (I'm reading these bullets from the crumpled syllabus in my backpack.) In most cases, his "gilded roster" shared these accomplishments with the world a full forty or fifty years ago. Ancient history, if you ask me... which no one ever does. The Jackal's special collection of "bright minds" are all male. They tend to've worked in groups of four, or in pairs. Many are now dead. They are almost always from England.

But what can *I* write for H-J-M's heartless homework charge today? This secret record with Robert and Håvi has been piling stress and guilt onto me, which is probably worth expressing, but no one wants to hear about that, and I find the prospect of writing music *about* music to be terribly dull. Plus, I'd rather die than come across self-involved. Can't a girl just sing in peace?

My attention floats from the interior of the passenger car to a mom-and-pop restaurant crunched in on both sides by a pair of new fast food chains. According to their marquees — bright, plastic signage that chokes the old family business between them from both passersby and sun — the corporations are doing great on sales. Thirty feet above the sidewalk, the train trundles forward, and in a split second, the image is gone.

Weeds, I scribble.

I sigh and nibble the end of the pencil. The commute is almost over. I should've finished this assignment at home. Anything can be a song concept, though, right? Thinking of the sixties, or any decade since, I debate simply writing the word "love" three times, then decide against it.

All the songs the Jackal teaches us are about girls, but I don't care about girls. I don't care about boys, either. If you ask Ingrid, I don't care about anything. More recently, now that we're "collaborating" on this album, my general lack of conviction has become a major concern for Robert, too. It also makes it difficult to drum up verses or choruses from inside myself, which I now have only four minutes to do.

Something occurs to me: if there's one thing I relish about public transit, it's the anonymity. That's a million times better than the scrutiny I have to endure riding in Robert's car. Whatever: I add a bullet point — slovenly and fast, it reminds me of a tiny black hole — then, *a place where no one knows who you are*. After thinking a moment, I jimmy the eraser into the bullet, nearly tearing the page, and round out a final answer starting to the left of the new graphite supernova: *the sweetness of a place where no one knows who you are.*

⌒

I check my phone and discover I have two missed calls from Robert. He's left a message, too. We've never spoken on the phone. I consider texting him, then remember he "doesn't text" — a stubborn resistance to any new business communication since literally before I was born. If that's a misguided loyalty to the "channels of industry" Robert used in the eighties, it's not worth reminding him he spent his own glory days representing pop artists with zeal and appeal tied to expensive synthesizers invented practically as their albums were being made. I know a little bit about this from Emily, whose enthusiasm for 1980's music once helped me distract us from one of our lessons. She shared it all without anything like Robert or H-J-M's condescension. Who knew? I guess every mentor has their passion point.

I look at the auto-transcript of the voicemail. There's no greeting — just:

Where are you?

Oh my god: I'm supposed to be at Håvi Håvsstrom's studio. Two nights ago Robert told me we'd scheduled a session for this morning. I revert to a little-kid state, suddenly the elementary-school girl who forgot to bring her piano books to a lesson, terrified of getting roared at by her mother in the car and met with only silence instead.

So now the girl who does nothing has managed to double-book herself, and if I don't solve the problem at hand, Robert may actually kill me. I can stomach lying to him; it's devising something this quickly that's the issue. I'll use the fact of commuting to music school this morning to my advantage. But based on our last two conversations in the car, on the pressure he put on me, I don't think he'll believe I genuinely forgot about the session. How unfair that I actually spaced out this time! I'm the girl who cried w —

Robert is calling again, and I don't have a choice but to answer.

"Hey," is all my idiot-trapped-prey CPU can muster.

Robert says it exactly like the transcript had sounded in my mind: harsh, direct and accusatory: "Where are you?"

"On the train," I say, uselessly. So far, though, so good: two seconds in, and I haven't lied. Yet.

"On the train," he repeats.

"Going to school," I qualify, meekly, afraid to deviate now, as though Robert can sniff me out over the phone.

"A renowned record producer and two adult musicians are sitting in a very expensive tracking room twiddling their thumbs because *you* told them you were available today."

"I forgot," I mumble — again, not lying.

"Håvi made the trek upstairs and out of the studio just to phone me." (This, to be fair, doesn't strike me as a huge deal.) "He and Jonny and that Indian guy have been waiting half an hour now."

"Ajay," I say, very halfheartedly.

I picture canid jaws cranking open and barely restraining themselves. More realistically, Robert is probably pressing his hand hard against his temple. "Mae, if I didn't know better, I'd think you weren't taking this record seriously."

"It's kinda your thing."

I hear a hard, vexed exhale — a vexhale. "Think of your mother."

"Ingrid's thing, then."

"Well, you can miss Grimm's for it today," he huffs. "Much of your tuition is covered with Håvi Håvsstrom's work anyway. Good thing I handled those records before you were born. So get off the train. And take the next one to the warehouse. Now."

"Wool... but school..."

"You don't care about school," he snaps. "You and I both know you only attend the academy to please your mother. Given your careless attitude, you can't be paying an iota of attention there. If she has faith in your talents, Ingrid has chosen not to see that. But I do. And I've never heard a single vocal exercise or an effort at songwriting bleed from the door of your room at home. I've let all that slide, because we'd both like to see Ingrid happy, or at least I pray you do. But it would be a shame if your mother had a stronger sense of how little you've invested yourself in music. Awfully spirit-crushing for her, I think, if someone made a show out of your carelessness."

But I do care about music, I think. I make a choking sound. "I don't have my songs with me," I manage. This is, very technically, not a lie: I always stuff all my music papers into the same backpack, which means the ones I stole from Robert's car are buried in there somewhere. But still — I don't have *my* songs with me. I never have.

"Well, you wrote them, didn't you?" he growls. "So you don't need to bring anything to the studio. Just do it from your mind."

"I..." but there are no excuses left. There's a hard lump in my trachea, but it's not barf this time. Rather, the hint of a sob.

"Hey," I say, unsure whether I'm about to plead or apologize, but I hear no encouragement, no response.

I refresh the screen: Robert has hung up.

A digital bell tolls, and a pre-recorded announcer says we've reached the next stop. I stand up. There's no recourse now. I've spent years fending for myself at the last minute, but that part of me is shrinking, and fast. I don't think I'm going to figure out a way out of this one.

February 20ᵗʰ (a Tuesday)
Mae

The train drops me off several blocks from the warehouse containing
Håvi Håvsstrom's studio, just before the industrial badlands of this part
of Chicago give way to partial forest. It's a good half-mile further than I
ever have reason to venture. Snow has begun to fall, and I draw my hood
up around me, briefly thankful the coat will make my presence obvious
to Håvi and the session musicians when I arrive. Then I remember
the studio is embedded deep within the building and nowhere near a
window. They won't even see me.

No one is around, and, shivering a little, I try Håvi using the phone
number Robert gave me. Straight to voicemail. I wish I had the other
musicians' numbers, but no one shared those with me. Ajay, Håvi had
said; a guitarist named Jonnny; maybe some people named Alex, but
Håvi said the Alexes won't need to join the sessions til we've knocked
out the first one or two.

By now I'm standing outside the imposing metal door and wishing
Robert had devised a way for me to reach Håvi more easily. I consider
calling Robert, but at this point I'm genuinely afraid to hear his voice.

I'm shivering harder and probably looking pretty miserable by the
time a wild-haired, scruffy-looking guy in a leather jacket bursts through
the door and props it open with a sizable rock nearby. The bags under
his eyes are a translucent black, whether from sleep debt or depression
or drugs or some Venn diagram of the three. He seems like a great fit for

this semiabandoned warehouse. If he wasn't so slight, almost dazed, he would nearly seem dangerous.

"You must be the singer," he says, clarifying things.

I didn't expect him to have an opinion about my identity. Why do people always preconceive who I am?

"I, um."

"Mae, they said?"

"Yeah."

"You look familiar."

"I get that a lot."

"Maybe your voice, too."

I wait for him to invite me into the building, but he doesn't. Why do so many musicians lack normal social graces? Robert and for some reason Ingrid have warned me about this phenomenon.

"I'm Jonnny," he says eventually. "Jonnny Rota."

"Mae Strand," I say, "but I guess you already know that." There's not a chance either of us is accustomed to this type of formality. He's pretending to be a grown-up, and I'm not even trying.

"We've been waiting inside for a while," he says. "Stepped out for some fresh air." He's fidgeting with something in his pocket. "D'you know your way in?"

"I came here a few days ago to meet Håvi Håvsstrom. I'm not very good with directions."

He laughs lightly. "We should've left a trail of breadcrumbs or something. That place is a mess. Not Håvi's, I mean. The warehouse." He produces a crimped packet of cigarettes, mostly empty. "That drummer, Ajay, left already. Said he has to work. Personally, I've got nothing but time. Would you tell Håvi I'm taking a minute?"

"Sure. And sorry for all the waiting."

"Blame the train."

"Factors outside my control."

"Exactly." He extends an arm toward the door. "Leave it propped, will you?"

I guess he wants to smoke by himself. "Sure." I push the big rock to the side, step through, and set it back, descending a grated set of steep steel steps under a bare series of bulbs, left to finish my return trek to Håvi Håvsstrom's studio alone.

For a few minutes, it's just me and Håvi down in the control room. I don't like this guy. That was easy to decide right away Saturday. He isn't likable in general, but he seems to have an even more intense idea of success for me than Robert and Ingrid. By now I'm weary and wary of this sort of pressure. Part of me wishes the nausea would surface just so I could get it out of my system during this in-between period before the session. But right now we're not talking, just sort of sitting there, so there's nothing to prompt it.

After a few minutes, Håvi asks offhand how my parents are doing. *What do you care?* I think. But I guess adults, even musicians, can have an instinct when it comes to passing time with small conversation. Maybe he knows about Robert's status in our house; I'm not sure how close they are. I elect to stick to my mother.

"She's fine, I guess," I mumble, feeling that mental locket reappear around my throat. "We don't talk too much, unless she's asking me about my music. She sleeps a lot."

Even this is me talking much more than I normally do, and I'm reminded of another nougat of Robert's advice: that producers sometimes have this effect on artists, probably through over-effort to make them ("us," I can almost hear Ingrid speaking on my behalf) feel at ease, or maybe because singing original lyrics can be so vulnerable. Probably the cause is people like Håvi Håvsstrom and Robert Koenid grasping at the inner voice of someone famous, or about to be. It's easy to imagine Håvi trying to squeeze and seize a rare intimacy with them ("us") in this way.

Feeling a vague pressure to say something, I add, "She floats around the house in this white bathrobe."

He nods, fingers steepled in front of his jaw. "Like a ghost."

"Exactly."

Jonnny, back from smoking, enters the control room.

"Well, we've been sitting here all day," Håvi says, rubbing his hands together. "It'll be easy for you to feel comfortable getting started with a smaller team. Why don't we take a look at the music? I have a keyboard set up in one of my tracking rooms downstairs."

"There's *another* downstairs?" I ask.

"For calm. Like clearings within this warehouse. The vocal booth is the most sacred. Today we'll use the larger room with that electronic keyboard and a few amp choices for Jonnny." He looks directly at me. "You've brought your songs, of course."

"My s — uh, yeah."

"Good, then! Let's head in."

As in a lesson with Emily, I can't help but start thinking of ways to stall before I remember we're killing much more than half an hour in here — that Robert is paying for this session, and that wasted minutes would likely be pinned on me. I envision the two sheets of paper I stole from his car crammed in the backpack I'm wearing, and I feel a wave of nausea. I turn to Håvi almost in a panic.

"Why don't you two start setting up Jonnny's stuff," I choke. "Håvi — can I use your bathroom first?"

"Meet us down in the tracking room when you're done," he says. "I trust you can find your way to the groves on your own."

When I pass back through the empty control room a few minutes later, my whole mouth is rancid, and I consider taking candy from the dish on the faux-wooden table to reset my palette. But indulging myself on Håvi's dime, even in the tiniest of ways, feels like indulging Håvi. I debate asking Jonnny whether I can bum a smoke, but I'm nowhere near cool enough to do that. I paw through the backpack and find nothing buried there. I produce both sheets of paper, then remember with another start I haven't looked at them since that hair-raising session in Emily's practice room. Maybe that handful of short glances across Emily's keybed will jog my memory this afternoon. Probably not, though.

So now, unable to stall any further, I'm seated awkwardly in the center of Håvi's primary grove. The large tracking room is much messier than Håvi's command center upstairs or than his description implied. A central rug underpins an electronic keyboard and a music stand, and Håvi has positioned potted plastic trees in a circle around it in some aggressive attempt at establishing serenity. Outside this dell, a rich undergrowth of cables springs up from every corner of the basement. I recognize them from Grimm's tech classes: every combination of ¼-inch and XLR cables, a box of pesky smaller adapters, a handful of power strips, all spilling outward like vines.

"Let's hear it," says Håvi, who has already resumed his relaxed, dominant position in a reclining chair just outside the clearing.

"Um," I say. I place the pages on the music stand. "Here's the intro..."

According to the sheet music, the first few bars are instrumental only, and I get through all eight of them without any hint that I don't know what I'm doing — pretending, effectively, I think, that they're my own. Are Håvi's efforts at curating a calm environment actually working on me? I suck in a shallow breath near the end of the section and am about to start singing when —

"I wrote that," says Jonnny.

The room goes silent. Håvi and I both stare at Jonnny, incredulous.

"I'm serious," he says, his eyes flashing. "I had to play each of those Chyrons songs about a million times on every tour. Couldn't stand them. Especially by the end. They're burned into my memory. Look."

He picks up the guitar and plays back the exact thing I've just done, note for note, change for change, everything a flawless recapitulation of my performance a moment ago — or vice-versa, I guess. The only difference is Jonnny does it faster, and whether this is his personality or that he's angry with me for stealing his music or that his knowledge of the song allows him to sear through it or the fact that the tempo wasn't indicated on the papers and I'd taken it too slowly, I can't say.

I find myself, once again, on the verge of throwing up.

"What's Chyrons?" I manage.

Clearly the question is as stupid as it was sincere. Jonnny snorts. "I was surprised from hearing that intro that you even know of Chyrons. You're so young. But c'mon." He gestures at the papers on the stand. "I came up with all those guitar parts for that band. Legally, I own as much of that song as the guy who wrote the lyrics. Or at least I should."

Jonnny looks to Håvi, who raises his hands: *Don't shoot me, I'm only the producer.*

Jonnny turns back to me, exhaust practically pouring out of his nose and ears. "You stole my stuff."

"Maybe it's a coincidence," Håvi suggests.

"Please. Listen to how specific these arpeggios are." Jonnny lays down the intro again, once again from memory, even faster this time, his possession asserted. Then he points to the sheets of paper. "Plus, those are handwritten, which proves they're not Mae's."

Håvi frowns. "You recognize your bandmate's handwriting from over fifteen years ago?"

"I remember a lot of stuff from my Chyrons days." Jonnny is now speaking as rapidly as he spits out his guitar licks. "Some days I swear they're still happening to me."

My seasickness swells again. "The lyrics are typed," I stammer, almost adding that someone must've copied them for some reason. "It's just the sheet music that's in pen."

"So?" Jonnny hisses, the "s" crackling like a flame. "Did *you* write them?"

I envision myself about five seconds into the future, spraying vomit all over Håvsstrom's special grove and thus needing to borrow money from Robert — who else? I might shatter Ingrid if I admit failure to her, and I have no funds of my own — to pay for the damages to the rug and potentially putting some strain on Robert's relationship with Håvi, adult pressures and balances beyond my comprehension, and I decide I can avoid all these things (though I know nothing about that last one) if I tell the truth about the charts right now.

"No," I mew. "I didn't."

Jonnny now looks weirdly smug for someone who's just been robbed while trying to rebuild his career. Håvi's massive sunglasses obscure whatever poker face is his reaction to the threat of explosion here in his sacred grove, a conflict hidden deep in a well beneath a well beneath the stairwells beyond the steel warehouse door in this woodsy part of Chicagoland. It occurs to me Håvi has probably watched artists fizzle and fracture and fight at one another's expense dozens, hundreds, of times down here. Maybe, to him, this is no big deal.

"Where did you find those charts, Mae?" Jonnny says.

I can't speak.

"She could have typed the lyrics herself," Håvi offers.

Jonny starts to glare — *I'm not talking to you* — then catches himself. Presumably he's earning cash for these sessions, and probably he wants recognition from Håvi too. "Yeah, maybe," he says. "But what about the handwritten staff paper? That's an important part of an important band's history, and it's sitting right there in front of us."

Important? Skeptical of Chyrons' foothold in cultural memory, I say nothing.

"Transcription," Håvi supplies.

I'm trying so hard not to get sick I can't open my mouth.

Jonnny looks so incensed I get goosebumps.

It dawns on me that Jonnny doesn't know about whatever work Robert is doing with Chyrons, since he isn't aware Robert is in possession of Chyrons material. Which means, if I give anything away, I'm igniting something bigger than I am. Suddenly this whole operation is starting to feel much more involved than Mae Strand's first album, or a gift for her mother.

So I stay silent.

"We're down here to make art," Håvi says, delicately. "So let's try not to worry about it, hm?"

"Not worry about it," Jonnny fumes, trying angrily now to meet my eye. I'm staring down at the keybed. "You stole, and you lied."

No one ever calls me out like this. If ever, it's Ingrid's passive-aggressive suggestion — or by Robert only recently, now that he has reason to bare his teeth. I don't really hang out with anyone else.

"She hasn't sung a word," Håvi says, gently. Over and above his financial interest in finishing this record, I sense something else, too, but Håvi is not the type of person to share his motives. It takes one to know one.

Håvi turns to me as seriously as a person can in sunglasses that size. "What songs *have* you written, Mae?"

I, keeping my eyes affixed to the keybed, continue to say nothing.

"*Do* you have any songs written?" Jonnny says, sharply.

I can't stall by saying yes, or I'll probably throw up, *and* they'll force me to perform something that doesn't even exist. I shake my head, pleading: "Don't tell Robert."

"Why did I come all this way just to waste my time?" Jonnny moans, setting the guitar down. "And you know what? I don't owe you anything, least of all keeping your secrets. You thought you could just bring a bunch of Chyrons songs in here and make the entire record like that and get away with it?"

"It was just one song," I whimper.

"Look," says Håvi. "All three of us want to make this record, right?"

Want has nothing to do with it. Jonnny needs the money. I need to keep my uncomfortable equilibrium with Robert so he doesn't make good on his threats to expose me to Ingrid — or something worse. And Håvi is bound to Robert in some past or present deal or a relationship that extends well beyond Jonnny and me. So we have no choice but to obey Håvi. *Non-negotiable* — that's how Prof. Stuart Hudson Jackson Margolis' course on Music Economics* would frame my position.

"Yes," Jonnny and I both admit in our odd new unison.

Håvi looks hard at me. "Well, Mae, the songs have got to be yours. The emotional benefit for our audience will be derived from your mind. From your heart. The originality."

"If she's unwilling and unable," Jonnny grumbles, "and if it's so important to you to get this album done, why not hire a ghostwriter? I'm sure a pro could write a batch of tunes well, and quickly."

"We can't bring in an outside creative," Håvi says carefully. "Robert was very clear on that. A third party might want the attention, the credit, and the money."

"Then why don't *you* write the songs, Håvi?"

Håvi shakes his head. "I've written hundreds of successful pop songs. I don't wish to write any more of them. I put my foot down, hard, on that side of the business years ago. I prefer my role as the producer. The decisionmaker." With a little irritation, he adds, "I've made this clear in a number of interviews."

As though reading my next train of thought, Håvi continues, "And no, A.J. can't take on any extra work. His other life is keeping him much too busy. It's going to be hard enough scheduling his sessions with you two. And the Alexes don't write. They're too squirrely for it."

I envision Emily, her boundless patience, her emotional bandwidth, her sheepdog's instinct to guide me to something good.

She'll help me.

---

* **Author's note:** Oxymoronic course name (1) unintentional, (2) unknown to Jackson-Margolis, and (3) unaddressed at Grimm's.

"I'll come up with something," I say.

Håvi looks pleased, but all I can see from Jonnny is a blank stare. Or maybe this is what he looks like when he's satisfied.

"How about a week from today?" Håvi suggests, standing up: today's session is over. "Mae, that should give you time enough to come up with something acceptable."

I nod as we exit the grove and make for the stairs. "Then you can both workshop the piece with me?"

Håvi laughs as we ascend. "Let's see how good the songs are before we decide to give *me* any songwriting credit." He smiles wryly, but I can't discern whether he's joking. His sunglasses are way too big for me to tell.

February 20th (a Tuesday)
Emily

Some people say water maintains memory, holds it inside, safeguards it, can transport it across places and peoples. This is how I feel about music — recorded music especially. Albums, after all, live forever. The artist communicates something permanent, etches their message and their soul into physical or digital material for good.

I wish our memories worked like that, but human recollection can't be stored on a hard drive and replayed in its original form, nor shared directly with a friend or collaborator, nor converted to different formats for our access or convenience. No: like water, memory shapeshifts depending on where and how it's kept, and by whom, and on the direction its natural body is headed. Maybe that's why people associate the two.

This particular morning, all the water around me is frozen in place, and my middle-class borough of Chicago is conspicuously quiet, as much for this early Tuesday hour as for the cold. I draw my gray wool coat around me with a shiver. It's beautiful out here, and still.

I've got both my dogs with me. The larger, Rubato, is pawing at a chunk of pebble lodged in an ice sheet. So named for his habit of moving around the apartment at an impressively random range of speeds, Rubato likes to take either a plodding clip or a full run without reason or warning.

"Fermie," I whisper to Fermata the smaller, who has a tendency to just... sit there. For as long as she likes. Which is what she's doing now.. "C'mon, let's keep it moving."

Walking the pair is a great opportunity to get some thinking done. And when it comes to reflection, I'm drawn much more toward the past than to the future. I like both, though. Actually, the fact of sitting with students one on one in that tiny practice room is one of the only things that keeps me in the present.

I usually have earbuds in during our walks. For several years, I've been adding most every song I enjoy to one massive playlist: "emily ultra," whose material spans seven and a half decades and whose genres criss-cross in just about every direction. There's no object of orbit — just stuff I appreciate, stuff I know. Part of what I like about the *ultra* playlist is that it deals very directly in memory, resurfacing it. When you hear the material, you're transported to the era of its release, even the location: the elemental English electric guitar tones of the sixties; the chewy, laid-back drum samples and needling sine waves of California nineties hip-hop; townsfolks' voice leadings in gainy midcentury Broadway records; the compression and untrained vocals of the impassioned 2000's pop-punk and emo of my very own Midwest; or my favorite palette, the shimmery keyboards and razorlike bell kits of eighties synthpop. And listening back reminds a person of when they discovered the song, of who they were at that time. Maybe when you "went through a phase" with the artist, giving repeated listens in bed or doing dishes or stuck in transit. Maybe you think of the person who showed you the song, or of some media buzz around releases in your own lifetime, or of some late-night rooting around Canonymous pages and pages and pages for noteworthy or long-forgotten pop and rock records, hunting for something new. At least I do.

I love this stuff, and it's part of my job to listen.

"Rubie," I say, gently but firmly, "let's get going." I can be assertive if necessary, but I never tug too hard on the leash.

⌒

"I need your help."

These are the words every music teacher, at least my ilk, longs to hear. Something in us is always awaiting a student who's interested, engaged, who's keen on the mechanics, the changes, the rises and falls within each phrase.

Mae has never fit this profile.

So, though she seems almost desperate when she enters my tiny practice room this afternoon — she'd texted to schedule a late afternoon lesson to make up for missing this morning without explanation, referring to this one as an "emergency" — I'm enthusiastic.

"So... *what* is this for?" I ask.

Because I encourage our sessions to flow like counseling, and because she'll take any opportunity to distract from lesson material, Mae has already explained to me her relationship with Robert. They have very little emotional exchange, but it is complicated: Robert lives in Ingrid's house (I experience a frisson just *think*ing that last pair of words) and has appointed himself something like Mae's mentor or impresario. Definitely not father. Financier, maybe. Lately it's pained me to hear that Robert has upped his pressure on Mae to take the business of music seriously, made her feel trapped and unhappy. For years, her mother has been doing the same thing. Still, some part of me is grateful: *some*one is pushing that girl to use her voice.

And it's a voice, timid though it may be in this tiny practice room, I swear echoes the voice of the artist my mother and I once shared. I'd remember that voice anywhere. What a gift that a version of it passes through a pair of adolescent lungs here in my very own workplace, boosted a little by my diligence as a teacher and by the vocal exercises Mae promises she maintains.

Since my mother's death, I've hunted for the artist's voice in record stores and thrift shops and every ragged edge of the Internet, but I only remember two discs: a small collection of songs, and those enchanting music videos. It's virtually impossible to track someone down when they want that badly to disappear. Maybe someone else, someone involved with Ingrid in the industry, wanted her to vanish, too. Who knows?

Perched beside me on the piano bench, Mae, meek and — until now — apathetic, has no idea where her own voice comes from. For invoicing purposes, before Mae and I actually started sessions, I'd had to take down Ingrid's first name from her initial emails requesting a Grimm's Academy music theory instructor for her daughter. After that, it took me a few instances of hearing Mae's singing voice before I connected the dots. For me, I hope those same dots will complete a constellation of some resolution, if only private and retroactive, between my own mother and my validation in music. (And, yes, a brush with fame. I'm only human.)

I'm so delicate on the whole subject, though, that Mae couldn't possibly know I know what I know about her mother. Whatever the reason for Ingrid's departure from an entertainment career some thirty years ago, it must be so... what? shameful? distasteful? unsavory? it's been kept from Mae her entire life.

I wonder how much this Robert — Ingrid's partner, recent addition to Mae's life, man of mysterious music industry insight — knows about Ingrid's fading away. Mae never cites pressure from Ingrid without including Robert's name. Maybe the whole mother-daughter wish fulfillment thing is my projection anyway. Robert does, or did, entertainment law for a living; I remember his name from a speaking schedule once posted by the academy. I have a feeling, with the strain on her increasing, Mae might mention this today.

"Emily?"

"Whoa," I say, laughing lightly. "I guess it's my turn to lose a little focus today, huh."

This scores a small smile from Mae. But she's clearly very worried, and I care much more deeply for her well-being than I do for approaching the truth about Ingrid.

"I think it's all a big plot," Mae says, and I physically resist my ears perking. "To get me invested in music. Professionally. This album. And now Robert says all the songs need to be original. Can you help me write one? You know so much about music theory, and you're so patient with me." She's breathless. "We already went to the studio. Not Robert — just me and a guitarist and the producer."

I cock my head.

"Some guy named Håvi."

My eyes widen. "Not Håvi Håvsstrom."

"You *know* him?"

"I mean, not personally. But he's very influential. I didn't even know he spent time in Chicago. I'd've assumed L.A. or New York. Or maybe Malibu. Or Stockholm, actually."

"Stockholm? Isn't that, like, in Europe?"

"The man is an electropop master. It's in their DNA."

"Well, his studio here is in some basement. A warehouse. I have no idea why he'd come to Illinois in the middle of winter if he lives somewhere sunny like California. Or interesting like Europe."

"Maybe he flew here just to work with you," I say playfully.

"...yeah, okay. Anyway, I showed him the same song I brought in here — the one that made you all disappointed in me."

"I wasn't disapp — "

"Turns out the guitarist was th — " Mae seems to realize or suddenly decide something, then stops. "He recognized the song. He knew right away it wasn't mine. Just like you did."

I nod, thinking of the age gap between Mae and me. "Chyrons. That was the name of the band. They did pretty well in the 2000's. Kinda forgotten now, though." Maybe later today I'll add Chyrons to "emily ultra" so someone remembers.

"Look, I need an original song," Mae says, clearly distressed. "Soon. Can you help me? Please?"

Ever striving to be a positive music influence, I push Mae to put in some of the work herself. "D'you ever scribble your thoughts down? On the train? Or in a journal on your bedside table? Things that pop into your head while you're counting sheep?"

Mae shakes her head. She looks almost frightened. This elevates my suspicions that Robert is some kind of predaceous music industry creature — and why not Håvi, too? Then a kind of wild idea strikes me. If we don't have time for me to show Mae how to write a song, I'll just give her one.

An option leaps to mind, one that tingles my childhood synapses. In the next few minutes, I can achieve three things, which I map in my head like an assignment for one of my younger students:

1. Obtain certainty that Mae does not know who her mother is. Once Mae has heard the song, her response should clear up that question for me right away.

2. Send a signal to Robert, by way of Håvi, that *someone* knows this record is somehow nefarious. By using Mae herself as the vessel for that message, I can avoid giving away Ingrid's identity to Mae.

3. Create the opportunity for me to hear Mae sing one of Ingrid's songs — an instance of star-alignment so delicious and rare I can't pass it up.

As far as #2 goes, I'm very resistant to stepping beyond the boundaries of my role in Mae's life. I don't know whether disclosing Ingrid's past to Mae would destroy one or both of them, or at least shock one half of the pair much more than anyone needs. I suspect it would.

Thanks to the power of the artist's recordings, the melodies and lyrics of one particular track are already banked in my memory, even if they've been forgotten to time and culture. This morning I can recreate Ingrid's chord changes by ear, just like when I was a little kid.

"D'you mind?"

Mae and I swap places on the piano bench. With a touch of nerves at the odd gravity of the situation, I sing and play through one of the artist's songs, "This Sugarcoat," in its entirety, stealing glances at Mae once or twice a section to see whether she's astonished or choked up or even angry. But she's just listening.

When I've finished, we sit in silence. Part of me is petrified Mae knows, is about to let on, is livid or at least offended at my theft. But she only looks... moved.

Finally, she says, "That's really pretty." Then a pause. "Did you write it?"

I've put myself in the position of lying, and I'm supposed to be a shepherd to my students, including to this girl who lies constantly. But at this point I have no choice.

I nod.

"Well, I love it," Mae says. I feel a rush and a peculiar comfort in Mae's *feel*ing the music, even if she doesn't know fully why. Maybe there's some inherent resonance in Ingrid's songs, one that bonds mother and child in some secret wavelength beyond all of us. That's what I imagine, anyway.

"Can you teach it to me?"

I glance at the clock and experience a vicarious pang of dread on Mae's behalf. "My next student is going to be here in five minutes."

She's still panicky. "Can you play through it again? I'll record it on my phone and learn it at home."

I can't have Ingrid — or Robert — overhearing the song while Mae puts it back together in the house. This would force Mae to explain where she'd gotten it, which would exacerbate the trust issues she's explained to me between herself and Ingrid and (respectively) Robert. It would also make it look like I'd asked Mae to give *me* the credit for Ingrid's hard work, which would be false and embarrassing. Moral failure, to say nothing of risking a swift end to my teaching career. Robert has *some* relationship with Grimm's, and who knows what strings he and his mysterious money can pull?

Then I remember to play to Mae's strengths. Music is deeply important to her — only in a way that Robert and Ingrid can't see. Probably because it isn't useful to them.

"You've secretive about your music," I say carefully. "You do it for yourself. Right?"

"Yes," she says earnestly.

"So you wouldn't want your mom catching any of it at home."

"Basically never, if I can help it."

"So you'll practice it when she's out of the house."

"Like *that* ever happens."

Ingrid's commitment to her own vanishing is tremendous. You have to admire it.

"Hmmm... Robert must take her on nice dates sometimes, right? Then you can make all the noise you want without feeling self-conscious. And no one ruins the effort."

"Wool, now we don't have time now for you to play through it again," she says, the pitch in her voice evincing that anxiety again. "Can you tape it and email it to me?"

"Of course," I say. "I'm sure I have your personal email from one of our lesson plans."

Mae stands up and balls her crimson coat under one arm.

"Thank you for today," she says. She's never signed off with gratitude before. Mae's sincerity, and her enthusiasm for the song, reassure me I'm doing the right thing with my own involvement. Even if there's a bit of mistruth involved.

When she leaves, I spend two minutes alone in my little practice room before my next student arrives, relishing the warmth.

February 20th (a Tuesday)
Jonnny

Here we sit again, down in the groves, twiddling our thumbs — or at least, butt parked in the control room sofa, I am. I've cooled a little. Twenty minutes ago Håvi encouraged me to step outside and enjoy a cigarette or two. It helped. You have to hand it to the professional: he knows his way around a collaborator's mood. Fresh air and a fixation fulfillment — that's relationship management for you.

Being unemployed, I don't share the awful time pressure Ajay clearly takes on from his work commitments. I'm also sort-of-secretly hoping that, in our few minutes alone together, the great producer will offer me more work. Maybe he likes me. Maybe that's why he called me for this recording project. Maybe he'll remember that now.

But now that we've leaned into this long day, killing time in one another's proximity, Håvi has been absentmindedly organizing his digital desktop, which faces away from me. He's deleting old production files or emails or something while both of us sort of hang there in the comfortable silence. All we can both hear, really, is the routine click of the mouse.

"I was thinking about you," he says idly.

Between two reserved men — Håvi's status puts him at a distance from most people, and I'm a depression case — of our generation, that's an intimate thing to say. Especially as we don't already know each other well.

"Um."

"The album with Mae," he says with the slackjawed distractedness of a multitasker. "Robert's idea. That's why I had you on my mind before I reached out the other day."

I want to encourage Håvi to think of me for session work, but I don't understand why I occurred to him this time or what some guy named Robert has to do with it. "...I don't follow."

The mouse clicks a few more times. "Robert," he repeats unhelpfully. "Koenid."

Unable to decipher his meaning, I stare at Håvi's shoulderblades, willing him to swivel the producer's chair toward me, in a reaction to my soundlessness, so we can have a conversation. Finally he does. He looks me up and down, probably reading the failure to register in my expression.

"You haven't met Robert Koenid?"

I definitely haven't. "He's, what, a lawyer or something, right? This thing was his idea — is that what you said? The album with Mae?"

"Yes, yes, of course." Håvi looks puzzled, but through his sunglasses, it's hard to tell. "I thought you would have met Robert by now, what with your collaboration. But maybe it's all taken place over the phone, email, I don't know."

"...collaboration?"

Håvi seems almost as lost by my inability to place the man as I am. Uselessly he says Robert Koenid's name again, this time like a question, as though simply inflecting his name upward will help.

"I don't... I don't have any use for a lawyer. I can't imagine why I'd need him. I mean, no offense to the guy. I just don't think I'd ever run into some attorney or need to work with him."

"What about the royalties, the placements? Television?"

At this point I can only continue to stare at Håvi. I can't help it. Maybe this seasoned producer has confused me with someone else. He's sharp — and I like to think my guitar parts stick in a person's mind —

but he's probably met a lot of people. Celebrities do, and he's gotten me conflated with another low-level not-quite-star or has-been. That's common in people of influence. Maybe, like time itself, Håvi has failed to remember Jonnny Rota.

"No, no," Håvi says, clearly certain I'm part of whatever he's talking about. "I know this from Robert. He's been working with you all for months."

"I'm sorry," I say, shaking my head. "Working with who?"

Håvi gives that authoritative laugh, fingers kneading one side of his forehead, amused by my apparent forgetfulness. "Chyrons, of course."

February 20th (a Tuesday)
Ajay

Ajay Chadhana is even more stressed than normal, which is saying something. In a few hours, he'll be performing with local hard rock outfit Sensory Overlords in the release party for their second album, *Heartbreak in Haymarket Square*, a big step in their relatively young career. Sensory Overlords' regular drummer bailed weeks ago for a better-paying gig, and Ajay had agreed to substitute for him just before Angie had disclosed the merger. In the flurry of all things S.P.L.I.T.- and Coldwell-related, Ajay did something he almost never does — forgot — to rehearse on his own. To've set aside time to practice with the band during the corporate cross-stitch would have been impossible.

If underprepared, Ajay has been equipped with an excess of detail from bandleader Bryant's overwrought emails, a phenomenon Ajay understands all too well from his own client messaging and from correspondence with his biological family. In the last week, Bryant has sent four production epistles whose granularity rivals even the bullet points populating the presentation Ajay has been hard at work every evening drafting for the higher-ups at S.P.L.I.T. and Coldwell.

In fact, Ajay has brought the halfway-finished presentation with him tonight, armed with the laptop Angie has "allowed" him to take outside S.P.L.I.T. headquarters for preparation and research in the increasingly dwindling hours he's not spending on software implementation project management during the day. Tonight's album release, here in the underbelly of the underbelly, is not the ideal setting for getting work done. For this crucial show, Bryant has rented Brokenhardt's, an improv theater often dedicated to standup and other forms of comedy. Standing outside the door, Ajay can already picture creatives younger than he, spewing rail drinks from plastic cups onto the blackened linoleum as they guffaw. He can't stand improv. Why give a performance that isn't meticulously prepared?

These, set within a splitting headache, are Ajay's thoughts as he heaves toms and snare and work computer backpack down a set of inky steps into the venue. Against the wall in the stairwell is a long and battered corkboard cluttered with flyers for arts initiatives and upcoming events: punk shows, comedy shows, touring acts' dates in town, meetups for social groups and poetry and urban agriculture and mental health. One is for some music school named Grimm's that boasts at least a dozen "industry alumni" on faculty.

Late in this Brokenhardt's afternoon, Ajay is the first performer to arrive. He likes this feeling, always has: not just being on time, even early, but soaking in the rare quiet hours of a place that's otherwise always clamoring with noise. Brokenhardt's lounge is awash with the acrid tang of citrus — some chemical cleaner meant to cloak the wet residual stink of cheap beer, of liquor on lacquer, of everything that will coat this countertop and floor in just a handful of hours. Later, the roar of the other patrons will be too unpleasant, too disordered, for Ajay to focus, much less enjoy himself. This feeling right now, the calm before the party, is one most bargoers will never know.

It's also a solidarity Ajay shares with his compatriots in the service industry, whose hustle he has always admired. He feels relieved to be spending time with people who won't judge him with the hard edge Ajay has grown accustomed to presuming of the tech world. In this case, the sole person downstairs is a rail-thin, bespectacled person about Ajay's age, clad in army green, stocking drinks into a refrigerator tucked below the counter and taking short breaks to wipe down surfaces.

"Ajay!" they say.

The bartender must recall Ajay from prior commitments: Eddie Momento's, perhaps, or Genuine Failures, or some other location(s) in their mutual underworld. Ajay has never made time for relationships outside work, though, or even within it. There's a guilt from failing to remember this person, but it's overshadowed by stress.

"Like 'a J,' but just one of them," the bartender says. "Get you a drink?"

God, does Ajay relish this part of the evening! Conversations are direct, questions audible, sentences complete. "Just the WiFi password for the green room," he says. "I'm trying to finish something up before we go on."

"Oh, there hasn't been a green room for years. Some restaurant across the street took up the space. Storage or something."

"Ah... is there Internet out here in the lobby?"

"We try to keep guests from using it so they actually pay attention to the improv." Oliver rolls their eyes. "Manager's rules. Not mine. Let me see if I can dig up the password for the private network, though. I'm only here once a week. Normally I'm at Genuine Failures across town. Oliver, by the way,"

"Of course," Ajay says quickly, repeating for himself: *Oliver*. He qualifies, "I used to play at GFC. In another life."

"You sure you don't want anything to drink?"

"If you could bag up a little ice for my forehead."

"You're not hurt, are you?"

"Just stressed."

Ajay finally sets his drums down in front of the bar, produces the S.P.L.I.T. laptop from his backpack, and flips its lid while Oliver sifts through cabinets below the counter for Internet credentials. Quite possibly Oliver grew up watching bartenders on television and in old movies, has been spending their adult life playing the part of one, and successfully, though Brokenhardt's is something of a dump. Hopefully, for both their sakes, the payout improves with ticket sales.

"The ice you asked for." Oliver plops the plastic bag down on the counter.

"Any luck with that network yet?"

"Just use my phone for the hotspot," Oliver shrugs, generosity coming easily. "We use it to run transitions for the comedians. Or just to screw around on the old computer back here if the performers aren't very good. I don't lose anything by sharing it with you."

This last sentence hits Ajay as exceptionally kind. Then Brokenhardt's' thick metal basement entry swings open, and a ragged man enters, wielding his guitar case with the same self-seriousness a midcentury businessman might his valise.

"Bryant," he says,* chipper. "You must be Ajay."

"That's right."

"Hey, why don't you set up your drums?" Bryant's intonation sounds more like an accusation than an invite, and Ajay wonders whether this Bryant, like so many artists with whom he's gigged over the last decade, believes his band to be the most important one on the planet. Or is Ajay just imagining things?

Pressing the makeshift ice pack harder against his temple, Ajay turns back to Oliver, pointing to the plastic bag. "Can you make this a double?"

Oliver nods and calls out to Bryant: "You want anything?"

"We've got too much to do. Too much to set up. Lot of people to impress. Ajay, can you help me with my gear?"

Ajay tries to meet Oliver's eye so they can roll them together, but Oliver is busy behind the bar. Ajay imagines responding, *Are you going to help me with mine?* But, as in Angela's office, it's easier to say nothing.

---

* **Author's note:** It's really neither here nor there, but this particular Bryant is the younger brother of Dave Starkey, one of the founding members and primary songwriters of Chyrons. Ajay will never have reason to learn that, though, so he doesn't.

Then he turns back to the bar, afraid he'll become angry if he tries to reply. "You know what, Oliver," he says, fishing for one of Angie's little white tablets in the very bottom of one pocket. "You don't have any energy drinks back there, do you? There's this one I've started to adore — it comes in a tall can, and it's blue and white..."

Half an hour later, in the Brokenhardt's storage closet behind the bar, Ajay is crouched on his drum throne, computer teetering on the pair of cardboard shipments of napkins he and Oliver stacked for him to keep preparing the S.P.L.I.T.-Coldwell presentation while the rest of Sensory Overlords shuffled into the venue and started setting up their instruments. Not wanting to seem uncool, Ajay hasn't told Oliver a corporate project (ick) is the reason he needs Internet and a semblance of auditory tranquility — just that he needs to be online to get some stuff done. He staged his own kit as quickly as possible so he could hole up here and focus. His first energy drink, and the ingestion of Angie's pill, helped with that. There's no outlet in the storage closet, and the machine is already precipitously low on battery, but Ajay is certain he'll be called for duty out there, to take the stage or for some other menial thing at Bryant's behest, before it dies.

He pops the tab on his second energy drink and takes a gulp.

The chatter outside is deeply annoying, but Ajay is able to direct his thoughts around the noise and sink them instead into research on his own company, spread across twenty browser tabs — not counting the separate window with just as many open pages of hypertension studies — and synthesize their findings for the pleasure and edification of the S.P.L.I.T.-Coldwell royal court. He's just settling into a groove with what he believes to be a particularly appealing set of bullet points when there's a rap at the door. This must be Oliver, whom Ajay has asked to serve as courier for anything time-pressured from Sensory Overlords. Sequestering himself seems like the best choice tonight; surely Bryant will hold against Ajay any implication that Ajay has something better to do.

The chemical combination has expedited Ajay's thinking even more than typically does his double-headed monster of anxiety and ambition. In a flash, he commits this moment to his memory: a heartwrenching little crossroads: in another life, even two or three years ago, Ajay would have been ecstatic to take this gig. Bryant, whoever he may really be, possesses real gumption, has sold tickets for a theater that, yes, if endemic to one mini-mini-ecosystem in Chicago comedy, curries respect in the creative undercurrents of this city. And an album release is a big deal for anyone. That Ajay got the call would have been a milestone in his early to mid-twenties. Tonight it's a millstone. That he could get by without rehearsing would have stroked his ego not long ago, but now he's just grateful it's given him the chance — here, tethered to someone else' computer in the Brokenhardt's storage closet — how did his life get to this? — to focus on his *real* job.

...which he can't do right now, because Oliver — sweet, hardworking Oliver — is knocking on the storage closet door with all their sweet, hardworking might.

"Yes," Ajay says, trying and failing not to sound irritated.

"The first band's about to go on," Oliver says, muffled by the layer of fake plywood between the two of them. "Bryant asked me to tell you."

"We're third, right?" *We.* Ajay restrains a scoff at himself, at his old habit. *I've been in this job too long*, he thinks. He is separate from Sensory Overlords. They are not like him.

"Uh-huh."

"Look, I'll just go out there when Sensory Overlords is up." Ajay almost says *on deck* and shudders. Was that golf or baseball? *When it's our innings*, he says to himself, a little more satisfied. Ajay's senses feel heightened, electric, and his heart is pounding hard. Tonight's internal tingling, ordinarily a source of fear and fixation, feels good. "You won't have to come get me. I can hear plenty from in here."

"No sweat," Oliver says.

Ajay feels a bead trickling down his forehead, and he presses the ice pack, now disintegrating within the plastic, to his brow again.

"You need more ice or energy drink?"

"Seriously, you're an angel." Ajay refreshes the screen. "More ice wouldn't hurt."

"You got it."

When the first band starts, drums and bass bleeding through the false knotted pine, Ajay's laptop informs him it's on its final battery reserve. Then he realizes his charger is nestled in the backpack he left tucked next to the drums onstage. The lithium should last until Sensory Overlords take the helm, but Ajay is afraid if the machine crashes during that time, he'll lose all his progress on the presentation, which he's unable to save to S.P.L.I.T.'s branded private "mountain cloud" from Oliver's phone's Internet, which doesn't pass muster for S.P.L.I.T. security. Since the secret announcement of the merger, internal company products are closed to most networks. And if Ajay's hard work gets lost or frozen, he's not sure he'll be able to control how livid he'll be.

He doesn't want to venture back to the Brokenhardt's throng, though. This reluctance is mostly out of concern for getting distracted, but also because he won't be able to stomach the proximity, the crush of these hard rock aficionados, especially if anyone elects to pester him about why, and to where, he keeps disappearing.

While the symptoms historically rear their heads in Angie's office, Ajay has been experiencing those hard twitches in his chest more and more lately — in the car, for example, when he has too much on his mind en route to S.P.L.I.T. or headed home; or at the living room table in his too-small apartment. This latter is a spartan work-from-home configuration whose sparseness leaves little room for ergonomics or any romance in design. But it does have enough space for the company laptop and sometimes a second screen. The low quality of his setup helps keep him focused. So he tells himself. Motivated. Hungry for something better — which is why he came to this country sixteen years ago.

Even with a robust corporate healthcare plan, Ajay wouldn't have time to get to a physician. Would he even be allowed to leave S.P.L.I.T. during the workday to see a doctor? And anyway, Ajay is certain the affliction derives from a binding-together of increased pressure and responsibilities at S.P.L.I.T., plus his body's aging — thirty looms only a few months away now — and genetic constitution.

Not to mention being high-strung in general. It is so, so hard to extricate self-worth from hard work, ego from achievement, success or happiness — who can say what those might mean? — and those from money. It's the weird tension of this dual life, of showing up at the S.P.L.I.T. office each weekday exhausted from gigging the night before, often past one or two a.m., having left those events prematurely for the same reason in reverse, mumbling some excuse about an early morning without letting on he'd be heading into a clean-cut corporate job. Creating and analyzing profit reports and managing implementation programs while the slackers take over the dartboard and the meditation room gathers dust a floor below him, shirt buttoned up to his neck for eight consecutive hours, his utterly *normal* sweatshirt slung all day over the back of his office chair.

Ajay takes a medium-sized gulp of the second energy drink, a step upward in speed and quantity from his judicious sips of even a few days ago. No wonder he feels he needs the guarana to get through nights like this one. He pictures the chemicals in Angie's little white pill crackling and dissipating within his bloodstream.

Now he hears applause from outside the closet door. The first act has just finished. Ajay realizes he could grab that charging cable from the stage and bring it back to his stopgap study before the second group begins to perform, so he moves quickly toward it, tallboy in hand, into the throng.

He runs into Bryant immediately.

"Where've you *been*?"

Ajay hears (or thinks he hears) a snap in Bryant's tone. If this is Sensory Overlords' big night, their leader is being anything but magnanimous about it. And the last thing Ajay needs is added pressure.

Retaining his coolheadedness, Ajay responds, "Am I needed for something?"

"Just be here. Validate our stagemates. Pay it forward."

"Ordinarily I would, but — "

"It's just one night. And it's *our* night. So let's show the other bands a bit more respect."

There's that firm ventricular yank again. Ajay takes another dreg from the blue and white can in his hand, hoping to quell or at least ignore the discomfort in his chest by focusing on the problems in front of him. Like most of the situations in Ajay's life recently, tonight's environs appear to leave him no choice. "Let me grab my backpack quick," he says. A small lie is permissible in placating Bryant: "My drum key is in there. I need it to finish getting ready for our set. Then I'll come right back."

Bryant eyes him up and down.

"Look," Ajay says, "if I miss a single note tonight, you c — "

Bryant exhales hard through his nose, nods with a resigned understanding, and steps away and onto something else.

A hotter-headed person might have challenged Bryant, but Ajay, even with stimulants and blue-number-five flooding his veins, had felt something akin to pity: the most Bryant could do to influence his behavior is complain. As Ajay sees it, he and Bryant have starkly different ideas about the American dream. Bryant wants to be notable — feels entitled to a little influence, to his circle's support in that endeavor. Ajay, on the other hand, is here to survive by hard work, and he can't outgroup himself for being "weird" on that subject, can't let his immigrant narrative differentiate him too much from these artists and artisans in their eyes, make himself unrelatable. Plus, he and Bryant are taking the stage together in less than an hour, so why start a row now?

Still, reputation matters. It's the crux of each of Ajay's cutthroat careers. Haughty under the surface, he'd considered informing Bryant how often he's appeared at big gigs like tonight's album release with precious little prep or presence and knocked it out of the park — no: nailed a hook shot — but managed to refrain.

For a moment, Ajay is left standing in the middle of the floor, constrained yet again by circumstance.

When Ajay takes the stage with Sensory Overlords, work computer safely ensconced behind the bar, he has Oliver's diligence and trustworthiness to thank. He clicks his sticks together four times, and things are actually off to a pretty good start. During the first two songs, no one looks at him funny. Anxious about recrimination from Bryant, Ajay keeps a watchful eye. He's been nursing his third energy drink effectively; he'd asked Oliver to pour it over a pint of ice, half to give the appearance of sipping liquor at the kit and half because the stuff is so much more enjoyable when it's close to freezing.

Several minutes ago, nested in the Chicago crowd, Ajay wasn't paying attention to the second act, didn't get their name, probably never will. He was working through the middle portion of the presentation in his mind, watching sales reports and earnings charts and pie graphs coruscate in dizzying circles around one another like cartoon birds around his head. By now, Ajay has practically finished the project in the space inside his skull, need only notate the remainder on "his" work computer fifteen feet away the second the opportunity arises, won't even wait to drive home and set up at the living room table, will probably hole up in the Brokenhardt's storage closet again when Bryant and the lot of them begin to celebrate the album's release, because he must keep momentum, best to strike while the iron's —

And now, on stage, Ajay's hands are shaking a little, but he practiced so much as a teenager he can play through any rudiment, any setback. Right? No problem. So sharply, too, did he hone his ability to memorize music in his early twenties he's still able to recall each section, each fill, each transition, from a cursory handful of listens to *Heartbreak in Haymarket Square* this afternoon — all in lockstep, for which he's responsible, and crushing it. More than once, he thinks, the bassist even smiles at him.

Ajay continues to take reasonable gulps of the energy drink during drum-free interludes or when Bryant is giving little monologues between songs. Under the stage lights, in its glass, out of the can, Ajay sees the energy drink for the first time in its true form: not in the clean, carefully marketed blue and white graphics one sees on clinical aluminum, but as a very poisonous-looking liquid, unnatural ochre fizz over ice cubes. Toxic. Angie's little white tablets, on the other hand, have been made to look so innocuous, so cleverly unassuming, so clean...

Ajay feels that hard lurch in his chest again.

Meanwhile, the presentation flits through his mind on repeat, now interpolated with animated images, flashing, unbidden: hollowed teeth, rotting bones, sagging clocks. He shudders. This reel, like some sort of subliminal ad placement, is just another thing he can no longer control. Meanwhile, there's a killer turnout — nodding heads, unfolded arms, earnest applause. Based on the energy here, Ajay can admit it: Sensory Overlords has something going for them.

Drumming his heart out, Ajay doesn't stop keeping perfect time — but, even while succeeding, he struggles to stay in the present. He's already affixed to the future, the presentation caked on his thoughts like Chicago frost creeping over the windshield of his crossover. He tries to scrape it all away, violently, with a physical shake. The chest pain is roaring now, and Ajay can no longer tell whether the jerks inside his chest are happening or are confined to his imagination...

Charging with all four limbs through the third chorus of a heavy-hitting Sensory Overlords track, Ajay looks into the crowd for hard proof of his surroundings, something to snap him back into reality. What he sees is incredulity and something approaching laughter writ large on their faces. In a rare effort to actually connect with his bandmates, he looks around the stage... and is stunned to see none of them are playing.

Ajay has botched the structure of the song, somehow overdone it, has been playing since the whole thing ended, and now he looks like an insane person, someone who can't stop flailing at the drums that enclose his body while everyone else on the altar is silent, gawping, frozen. He rounds out the last bar, flourishing grandly at the very end, and sets his sticks down, panting, hoping for a split second this awful moment will come across as irony, a poorly executed joke, somehow intentional. But there's no façade. Bryant turns around and faces Ajay, looking like he might explode. Perhaps he'll finally lose his high ground, heaving his guitar down on the stage and pelting Ajay with expletives. Perhaps he'll inform Ajay and the crowd that Ajay has ruined this special night with his low level of preparedness beforehand and attentiveness during it. Perhaps the crowd will be transfixed, entertained, because they'd be getting a much more interesting show than the one they paid for. Ajay starts to think if one person here would vouch for him, it'd be the army-green angel behind the bar, but what could they possibly say to redeem him?

Ajay's heart is pounding up to his ears; his neck and shoulders and armpits are soaked in sweat, the angina so severe it's fused with his very being — not a sensation, far beyond a fear, *part* of him, now, and what happens next, he's sure, is not the product of embarrassment or panic or of tossing back two and a half venomous energy drinks in just a couple hours or of Angie's tiny pill or of running himself completely into the ground the entire last week with the stress of putting this presentation together or of the sheer pressure since childhood to achieve so highly in two separate fields with so little time in a day — but of genetics, of his physical size and phenotype, of one of very few things actually *given* to Ajay his entire life, in fact even before it began: that bridge between his hereditary makeup and his hypertension. He can picture the articles, can practically recite their findings verbatim, suites of factors entirely beyond his control.

Ajay feels himself falling to the floor, hears the sticks clattering what feels like oceans away, and watches the edges of his vision start to ebb and blur like a big bang in reverse. Finally he experiences a great wave of something he hasn't felt at this extremely high level since bolting around the cricket pitch at fourteen under a Jamshedpur sun:

Heat.

"Bryant," he croaks. "Oliver. Somebody. Call an ambulance. I'm having a heart attack."

February 20th (a Tuesday)
Jonnny

While my quality of life has been getting lower and lower, the old Chyrons guard have been busy colluding with Robert. How can I, in my car outside the warehouse of Håvi's studio, be so confused and so livid all at once? Is their relationship a coal worth stoking further, or better left to extinguish on its own?

I elect quickly to poke at the embers. Chris and Other Dave are almost certainly unreachable by now. It would never occur to me to dig them up on social media, and I'm sure their numbers have changed since 2009. So the only person I can feasibly reach is Dave, and only because the name of his record store in Pennsylvania is stuck somewhere in the craptacular votive of my memory. What's the difference between the act of recollection and living in the present? It's all happening in your mind at the same time anyway. I look up the business' phone number and try it. I'm greeted by a monotone drawl: "Fallen Star Records."

I haven't really thought about what I'm going to say; the whole idea was less a plan than a fiery impulse. "Dave around?" I manage through clenched teeth.

"Yeah, can you hold?"

Let's be honest: not usually.

Distant, metallic audio — the time-killing kind — passes through the speaker, the fidelity so low it's like vinyl is being spun and broadcast here from outer space. Then a gruff male locutor answers: "Dave here."

"You're not gonna believe who this is! It's Jonnny."

There's a brief, awkward pause.

"Jonnny Rota," I try again. "From Chyrons."

There's another hesitation. My mistrust skyrockets.

"Jonnny," he says blandly. "How are you."

"I thought you might be more excited. It's been, what?"

I picture Dave shrugging. "Thirteen, fourteen years."

"Crazy, huh?"

"Crazy. So what's up."

Without a plan of action, I simply speed ahead. "You work with Robert Koenid?"

There is, for the third time, an infuriating pause. "We don't have any 'Robert.' Not on the floor, anyway. Maybe sales? He a distributor?"

"Robert Koenid," I repeat. "He's an entertainment lawyer."

I can practically see Dave's gears turning, devising explanations, excuses. He laughs uncomfortably. "Well, we don't really have a use for any entertainment lawyer here."

"I mean for Chyrons. For whatever you and Other Dave and Chris have been plotting."

"*Plotting?*"

I'm grasping a little, but what else am I going to do? Hang up now and never know? Take the Swede at his word? "Royalties. Placements. I don't know."

"Look..." he says. "The three of us have been *talking* with this lawyer. Robert, you said. Koenid. Just to make sure someone was keeping an eye on Chyrons streams. Monetizing them. From the few fans still out there. And maybe he did a little sync work, too."

Heating up physically and hoping my silence serves as a useful trap, I wait for Dave to explain. When I first bought the jalopy — I don't know how many years ago — I learned the negotiation tactic that if you simply say nothing long enough, the other party might feel pressured to say something that doesn't do themselves any favors. This actually seems to work:

"One of our songs caught the ear of some TV exec working on a *best of the aughts* series. It's a retrospective or a documentary or whatever. They're gonna put the track in the background of some interview clips of 2000's tabloid stuff or montage or something."

"One of our songs," I repeat, incredulous.

"It's digital infotainment, dude. Directors and producers cashing in on people's nostalgia. It might not even get any attention, or streams, or clout, or whatever."

"Why wasn't I consulted?"

"Look," Dave says again — patronizingly, which makes me even angrier. "It'll probably just be playing really quietly under paparazzi photos from the era. People way more famous than we ever were." He clears his throat awkwardly. "Plus, you don't have songwriting credits on any of that stuff. Me and Chris and Other Dave had everything together by the time you showed up to the party. Before the talent scout, from, oh, what was the name of that label."

"Weedbills," I say, now seething.

"Weedbills. And you were fine at it, but you were younger, and, y'know, you were a hired gun."

This gun is smoking hard. "So there's no way in for me now?"

"Look," he explains in the same aggravating tone, "All the mechanical royalties... at the end of the day, the larger percentage goes to me. They're my songs."

"What about the payout I get every few weeks? Royalty checks?"

"It's a good deal for you. We figured, to be nice, we would keep sending something your way, y'know, in perpetuity."

"...like charity."

He sighs. "You were so young when you started with us. We figured it was the right thing to do."

I picture my crappy apartment, dirty dishes, broken guitar strings, old mail on filthy surfaces. My current surroundings — the jalopy — are no good either: multiple maintenance lights have been blinking for weeks, and the gaslight just flickered on. Fast food wrappers have been unraveling themselves in the space before the shotgun seat. A smudged copy of outdated insurance paperwork is crumpled uselessly in the console. "Lot of good that did me."

"Look, I gotta go. I still do a lot of work at the counter. You should really come by the shop sometime!"

Dave's empty graciousness stings even harder than Chyrons' false goodwill, and there'll be no way to reach Dave or the other guys — the option of calling again after some time has passed is too shameful for me — as soon as he hangs up.

...which he does.

Asshole!

Now I only have two things on my mind: trust and money. I don't even set my phone down before ringing Håvi.

"Yah," he says. He sounds like he's sucking on his own stash of the jawbreakers he keeps in that stupid bowl in the control room.

I pivot to my sweetest tone, hoping it's convincing. "I want to thank Robert for putting this record together," I say. "I think a handwritten card is the best way to go. D'you have his address?"

Snow is falling heavily when, just a few minutes later, I'm careening dead south toward the address Håvi gave me for the Wolf Lodge, a hotel that isn't too far from Håvi's groves. It's supposed to be about a twenty-minute drive.

To prime myself for the confrontation, I've put on one of the few CD's in my console: the second and final Chyrons album. *If Bedlam Stirs*. Not the best acronym, and I haven't revisited these collections in a long time. Why bother? The songs don't do me any good, and I remember most of the parts like the back of my hand anyway. Take something on the road that many times, and it'll always be seared into your memory.

You might think I would be exposed to the *Bedlam* recordings tonight and be swept with emotion, hardened by bitterness or softened by nostalgia. But instead I feel nothing. I only *hear* the music. Everything outside the jalopy is muted by the mounting snowstorm.

Pushing my old vehicle well over the speed limit, I'm rotating an album from over a decade ago, on my way to accost a man I've never met, regarding events I wasn't a part of. I start to wonder whether anything in my life is, has been, real. My crappy apartment — that's real. The physicality of my guitar — that's real, too. A wrathful digestive tract — that's definitely, painfully real, though I can almost hear a physician asking me to be honest with myself about how many of my urges are psychosomatic. My constant lack of funds — that's not really real; it's a gap where something ought to be. But it's just as real as every other facet of my life.

The most present part of my life is my past, and I just learned that's not real, that the friendships within my Chyrons career were a sham. For another thing — especially for someone like me, who's steeped in it — maybe you shouldn't trust memory. And you definitely shouldn't trust people either.

And if you can't rely on people, what *do* you have? I consider my less-fond moments in the Chyrons van, which, now that I think about it, was most of them, especially near the end: my own perceived need for various stimulants just to keep pace with the energy between Chris and Dave and Other Dave; and the unrelenting roasts from the rest of the guys those few short years as I singled myself out with increasingly plaintive calls to stop for a bathroom. I was the runt of the litter, not fully one of the gang, not a whiz kid or a gifted kid so much as... just a kid. I have a theory those gastrointestinal urges came not from a childish lack of impulse control but from the very opposite: from getting older —

from a system already failing me at seventeen and destined to continue doing so at higher and higher rates of malaise and desperation until my last hours on this sad, weird planet, of which I've always had a strong feeling there aren't many left.

As I race through tonight's blizzard, the hot smoke of my anger with Robert, with the entire Chyrons faction, with the situation, with myself, with my past, has all fused into one great all-consuming plume, and a really spectacular idea occurs to me. Why not abandon my mission at Robert's — abandon everything, in fact — and drive the jalopy off of one of these bridges right now? With one very hard right turn, I could easily plunge the car into the Chicago River and deposit my physical, mental, and financial ailments into the half-frozen body of water for good, and quickly. Or, even easier: I could simply pull over, cut the engine, and let tonight's minus-zero climate quell my anger forever.

The snow is coming down so thick I can barely see the road ahead of me, much less maneuver to the shoulder and commit my most extreme act of self defeat to date. But I don't slow down. Whether I attack Robert tonight (verbally) (...probably) or put an end to everything, I want it to be done. And fast.

Still, I have no desire to put a stranger at risk. It's the people you trust, after all, who will screw you. So I fixate, as throughout my life, on the rearview mirror. No one appears to be inhabiting my blind spot, and, pushing seventy, I bring the vehicle even further left, taking over the fast lane, passing room be damned. I've been letting the people around me eclipse me my whole life.

Visibility being what it is, everything blanketed, I can't tell whether I'm crossing the median or headed towards oncoming traffic, but it doesn't matter. Thinking I see a little blur coming from the other direction, more like a phantasm than a car,* I swerve to avoid it, and, as

---

* **Author's note**: Jonnny is unaware the sedan trudging directly toward him, due north from Robert's, happens to belong to Ingrid Strand. Bound homeward from her own evening at the Wolf Lodge, Ingrid is driving as lethargically as she lives, plodding but determined to sleep in her own bed.

throughout my life, I don't realize what's happening to me until it's too late. Without warning, without visual cue, my vehicle spins fistfuls of times, in mad circles, finally slamming against the guardrail opposite the median, sixty feet above the Chicago River.

For a moment, every piece of sensory intake looks, sounds, smells, tastes and feels like fireworks. It's beautiful. Then, here at the edge of the bridge, neurological signals give up on firing correctly, and everything I see is black. This must be my own ocular field narrowing and failing as I lose consciousness forever, or else the Chicago River subsuming me and my crappy car. Then everything vacillates to total white: all-enveloping snow, falling relentlessly the only way possible:

Downward.

With what little strength I have left, I reach outward — as throughout my life, I have no concept of which way is up — and finger my way to the audio power button on the dashboard. I thumb it, hard. The music stops, and, for once, I exercise gratitude. It would be unthinkable to die while listening to Chyrons.

February 21st (a Wednesday)

Jonnny

mae ill be honest. i dont trust u, u stole
my hard work & tried to pass it off as ur
own to a industry powerhouse, maybe its
ur youth & inexperiance no offense but
u should really get that checked out ur
tendency to lie i mean

got ur email address from havi, told him
i wanted to send u a few pre production
notes. fine, once in awhile i guess i can lie
to.

i had a revelation lastnight the bridge,
i was going to dosomething terrible but
someone elses car forced me out of it,
first stroke of luck thats happened to me
since my career began.factors outside my
control i guess

writing frommy phone in a hospital bed
down town,mild injurys they said 'time will
heal' , the iv they have me plugged in to
has great stuff init & i have nothing todo
but type so t , bare w me, also it feels

like i passedon & came back to life & just
needto tell someone. so if u dontknow any
ghosts already, now u know me

u should getout while u can. the music
business i mean but definitely this record
w havi to. seriosly. look at me, all my pride
all my glory is inside of memoriesfrom a
decade & a half ago.plus i dont havea
whole lot of miles left in me, i have a
strong gut feeling about that.

ur not doing this thing (ur career in music
for its own sake ur doing it for i dont know
some constraints put on u like a cursed
almost pressure fromrobert to succeed.
maybe condesending but if u want to do
it (music & if u stay in it, u needto stay for
the right reasons, putting ur whole ego into
1 basket can be a nasty endavor & the
crash at the end is notworth it trust me

personaly i had 2 reasons to for staying
in the game kinda mixed up together
my self worth & the recognition/ acclaim
even if they were not that huge & once i
got used to the 2nd one i lost the 1st one
as soon as the 2nd one went away. that
was 15 years agowhich makes the pain &
separation & like ego death? feel almost
as old as i waswhen my guitar career got
started

think of it thisway music for people like us
is a sickness. the veryfew people i admire
had the intuition, ur voice for example &
desire to pursue music for its own sake
so not just wanting itfor external reasons
but self pressure- disatisfaction- or
compullsion. like we have no choice but to
go through w it

u have that first trait mae but u dont have
the others, i saw it down in the groves.

u could develp them but why would u
tangle ur value as a person w something
so.. fickle w high chances of comercial
disapointment w so much potential to
make u..miserable

the rare ones i look upto they all seem
to inter twined their guts their spirit to the
music completely & i cant tell if that inter
twining makes them happy /confident /
stable whatever certainlynot rich but how
could u possibly make it otherwise, or is
that typeof person simply cant do anything
else

who knows maybe u are i areboth
unhappy people. maybe its just that
simple. maybe regardless,we will always
be that way. maybe im just projecting

the cost of ambition im tryingto say it
hardens ur heart thats obviosly what
has happened to thatguy aj not music
necesarily but whateverjob has him
doing emails off hours & on weekends &
stressing out all the time. may be u ever
met theguy but im ucan imagine the toll
every competetive forces u to bottleup this
hard type of intenseness thatsays if u think
im not the real thing whatever thatmeans
then i will prove u otherwise & ill deal w
the setbacks to my own hapiness later.,is
that a ball ofyarn u really wantto bat
around forever

i forgive you for the theft btw, thats me
sending this email, the peaceoffereing is
my advice to quit the musicgame. ur still
yong. & if im being honest i don't have
high expections of runninginto u again so
unless some weird turnof events has us
crossing paths in thefuture i supose this is
goodbye.

so be well & seriously find a way out of
that record w havi

all my best- or whats left of it

jonnny

February 21<u>st</u> (a Wednesday)
Mae

It's been forever since I last camped out in the practice room in my mother's basement, and I'm not even sitting at the piano. I've positioned my laptop on the messy counter surface across the room, and I'm about to open the attachment Emily had promised to track and send after this morning's session. She's included a note of encouragement — "You can do this. For yourself" — plus a reminder, now her third, not to let Ingrid or Robert hear so much as a snippet. Easy enough: Ingrid is always hiding out in her reliquary at the top of two flights of stairs. And if Robert is even in the house, he's up there with her (ick), or he's ensconced in the study he'd set up for himself almost as soon as he and Ingrid started spending time together this fall.

My inbox also has a message from Jonnny, but I don't read it. Lately I'm learning I don't need to pay any mind to what these other musicians think of me. It's my own journey that matters.

Dispelling thoughts of all three of those people, I don my headphones and take a listen. The file is titled "this.sugarcoat.m4a," and I enjoy Emily's composition, even through her tinny phone recording. To my ear, the wonderfully simple chords fall under straight-ahead pop covered in various theory classes at Grimm's (H-J-M: "timeless mechanics"), which Emily's thoughtful reference guide confirms. Very pretty, and nothing too complicated, they might as well be from any decade. Emily has also included the lyrics. I like them. They're evocative. Until this morning, I didn't even know she wrote her own music. I guess everyone is full of surprises.

I listen twice, figuring I'll then sing the whole thing alongside Emily's track in my headphones. Once I'm more familiar, that'll be much easier and quicker for me than working it out at the piano. After going through the song aloud a few times, I should be able to remember it for the purpose of presentation to Håvi — and Jonnny, and Ajay — a few days from now. Hopefully I can do that with a confidence that'll convince them its origin is Mae Strand, Chicago's Fledgling Creative Talent Who Totally Cares About This Project.

I sing "This Sugarcoat" once, mumbling a little and pausing in a few spots to get the melody right. I feel awkward, even though I'm perfectly alone down here. The only times and places I really sing are when I have the rare opportunity to drive the Strand "family" vehicle by myself, and even then, that's usually en route to pick up Robert from one of his meetings. Even in those cases, I have his presence hanging over my head. The basement is acceptable, and isolated I suppose, but the very fact of its being in Ingrid's house makes me feel less than 100% comfortable vocalizing here. After all, she never leaves. Plus, for months, Robert has made this place feel like his house, too.

But during tonight's solo rehearsal, the song is already starting to feel pretty good. I sing through "This Sugarcoat" a second time, now with increasing self-assurance — something that has never come naturally to me. How could it, in this house, under all this pressure? Feeling bolder, I add a tiny vocal run to one of the choruses, then exaggerate a little dynamic ebb and flow in the second verse. I explore the vowel shapes I learned in my first year at Grimm's, ones I'd started finessing on my own sometimes in a private practice room but mostly in secret, in a bathroom mirror at the end of a forgotten hallway between classes. Tonight, so far, I'm pleased with the outcome. Maybe a college degree actually has some value.

End to end, I sing through "This Sugarcoat" a third time, now able to perform it for myself with less consciousness, less meticulousness. I'm proceeding instead by a method I much prefer: by instinct. By feeling. At this point, the chords and melodies and lyrics have seeped further into my bloodstream. I might actually be okay at rehearsing, at *work*ing, which for me is truly unprecedented. This interpretation of the song — it's starting to belong to me.

Headphones still on, I'm in the middle of my fourth run-through when something in the room starts to feel off. For now, I ignore it: to my surprise, I'm enjoying myself. I believe I'm in what various Grimm's instructors have described as a "flow state." Until this moment, I'd never thought that was a real thing. So I finish this pass, eyes still glued to the laptop screen, ears still attuned to the headphones. It feels good to plug into this effort completely. My voice, finally comfortable in the Strand residence, is growing louder, fuller, more expressive. I'm developing. I'm learning. Even when I report this progress to Emily, that external reward will be secondary. This — this is for me. For the first time in my life, my effort feels gratifying.

I finish this rehearsal of "This Sugarcoat" and, removing my headphones, finally look around the room, hunting now for the source of that negative aura. When I see it, my heart takes a frighteningly hard thump, and a chill scampers across my shoulders. Draped in her white bathrobe, leaning against the doorway, backlit by the crummy bulbs in the hallway behind it, there she is.

Ingrid is watching me intently, and not with that catlike depressive half-droop to which I've been accustomed for years. No — now her eyes are wide open. And she's been *listen*ing. Instead of complimenting me, or giving unsolicited vocal advice, or pushing me, or correcting me, or whatever else I might have expected, my mother tells me something I would never have guessed:

"I wrote that."

February 21ˢᵗ (a Wednesday)
Ajay

Ajay Chadhana awakens slowly, supine on a time-beaten couch. Linoleum commands his field of vision, stale beer rankles his nostrils, and someone is standing over his body. For a moment, he thinks it's a medic. Then an angel. But it's Oliver.

Ajay rasps their name.

"Hey," comes the gentle response.

"Wh — where am I? What happened to the rest of the show?"

"Everything's gonna be fine," Oliver says. "It happened already. You're still at Brokenhardt's."

In a fog, Ajay attempts to swallow. "W — water, would you?" He hears foraging in the cabinets nearby. He feels everything in his body. It's awful. "Oh, god — my work computer."

"*That's* what you want? After everything that happened?"

"I was way behind on something, and I'm supposed to be at work today, so — "

"It should be next to you. Thankfully someone at the show had nursing training. I have no idea what a professional *any*thing was doing at Brokenhardt's on a Tuesday."

"What about my drums?"

"Bryant and I packed them up for you last night. They're back in that storage closet."

Ajay's head is killing him. "D'you have any coffee here?"

Oliver winces. "I'd almost be afraid to make some. I think last night was because of all those energy drinks."

Ajay thinks of Angie's pills, how he has one left in his desk drawer at home, but pushes that thought away. He unzips his backpack, produces the laptop, and flips its lid. "Let me get back on that hotspot quick."

Oliver groans. "You didn't have a heart attack, in case that matters to you."

Ajay opens the presentation to ensure his progress hasn't been lost. Absently he says, "That's good."

"The nurse-person said those are 'exceptionally rare' for people our age. You're probably, what, thirty?"

"Mm."

"They kept calling a heart attack a — " Oliver pauses to refer to the back of an order ticket, where someone has dictated or scribbled the nurse' assessment " — 'myocardial infarction.' They said that's *not* what you had. Could've been acid reflux. Or" [reading again] "*stress-induced pe ri card-it-is*. That one they call a 'tissue issue'."

Ajay flits through the slides a second time just to be sure the presentation has been automatically updated and saved.

Oliver exaggerates a sigh. "D'you seriously not care about your own health?"

Ajay presses the glass of water hard against his forehead, grateful for its frigidity. "Look, I just need to email or message my boss and come up with some excuse for being offline all morning. Then I'll be out of your hair."

"You had a frickin' cardiac event, dude. Or a major muscle thing. You passed out in public. That should give you plenty of latitude with your job." Oliver shakes their head, incredulous. "Why don't you just tell them the truth?"

"I don't like to shed light on my double life," Ajay tries to explain. "It's corporate."

Oliver can't help but laugh at the absurdity. "See, we didn't even know whether you had healthcare. That's why you're still here and not at a hospital."

"It's a time of transition. Very cutthroat. Little empires. Could be very pivotal for me." He stifles a yawn. "I don't need the company higher-ups to know my mind has been somewhere else."

"I find that very sad."

Ajay drains half the icewater. "Are *your* coworkers creative people? Do *they* have other lives?"

Oliver laughs. "I'm a bartender at a comedy club. What do you think?"

Ajay lifts his gaze to Oliver from the S.P.L.I.T. computer for the sole purpose of arching one eyebrow.

"Every coworker I've ever had has an alter ego. Side projects. Fantasies. Big ones, even."

For the first time since firing his old friend, Ajay pictures Fred. "See, not a luxury I have."

"Luxury." Oliver chuckles. If they have another life, or a half-dead dream, they don't promote it to Ajay now. "You seriously need to reorient your relationship to your work."

Ajay toggles the mouse to keep the laptop's pinwheel from spinning.

"You should take the day off," Oliver suggests. "See if an urgent care clinic will let you in and look inside your chest. At least get something for the stress so it doesn't happen again."

Ajay puts the glass to his forehead for further cooling before realizing he's emptied it already. He thinks for a moment, then hammers out an instant message to Angie:

Been heads-down on preparing S.P.L.I.T. / Coldwell presentation
Will keep working remotely to stay focused

He adds, *Quiet here*, then sends it.

"Take your time getting up," Oliver says kindly. "We don't open til this afternoon."

⌢

Sitting down at the kitchen table in his too-small apartment, Ajay's first thoughts are not to head straight to a clinic, nor to make an appointment with a specialist, nor to physically relax, but of the emails he needs to send. First, to let Bryant know he won't be taking any more Sensory Overlords gigs. No qualifiers there; Ajay's embarrassment was apology enough. Strike that, actually — there's no chance Bryant would ever hire him again. Second, then, in good conscience, is to cancel with the people involved in that recording project. The album that hasn't happened, with the vocalist who never showed up. What was her name? Mae.

Having neither Jonnny's nor Mae's email address, and unsure whether Håvi's alleged Alexes even exist, Ajay begins to write to the producer.

> From: Ajay Chadhana
> Sent: Wednesday, February 21, 2024, 12:31 PM CST
> To: Håvi Håvsstrom
> cc:
> Subject: Recording Project
>
>
> Good afternoon, Mr. Håvsstrom,
>
> I hate to be the bearer of bad news, but I suppose it is my bad news to bear. Due to increased pressure on my schedule,

Ajay elects here to cite neither last night's health scare nor the deepening schism in his time and attention between the music career and what his biological parents might call his *real* job. Only one of the two brings income into this too-small apartment, justifies their facilitating Ajay's journey to the United States, doesn't pale in comparison to Ira's legal career. Anyway —

I am no longer able to invest my time in
preproducing or recording drums on this
record with the young vocalist, Mae. Prior
commitments cannot be moved. Nothing
doing! If you would like help finding and
onboarding a substitute, I will be happy to
make use of the referral resources I have
prepared on account of my busy schedule.

Given his recipient's industry experience, Håvi's sure roster
of contacts, Ajay's offer to track down and ingratiate personnel is
unnecessary. But it's a more gracious exit than simply dropping out.

Thank you for including me in the process
thus far, and do not hesitate to reach
out if I can provide further assistance
with firmware, plugin reconfiguration, or
installation at your studio. On behalf of the
S.P.L.I.T. team, I am always happy to help.

I hope we have the opportunity to work
together soon!

Best regards,

Ajay Chadhana

Software Implementation Project Manager

S.P.L.I.T.: Project planning promoting
private parties' primary processes,
products, profits, people, platforms and
propositions since the late 90's.

Thinking he's finally approaching the finish line, Ajay turns back
to the slide deck, hoping not to let his growing personal woes inhibit
his productivity. This'll be the rest of his day, pericarditis be damned.
People say it's isolating at the top, but he still feels nowhere near the
peak.

February 22<u>nd</u> (a Thursday)
Ajay

With the aid of several energy drinks and one more of Angie Miller's tiny white pills, Ajay has stayed up all night to finish the presentation for her critique, of which there hopefully won't be much. The only instances in which he's gotten up from his ramshackle work-from-home kitchen table in the last eighteen hours have been (1) to step out to the bodega in the middle of the night to restock on those sweet, sweet blue guarana tallboys, during which errand, in a rare act of impulse, he purchased a bag of cherry sours. Owed perhaps to his corporation-induced fugue, the shape and color of the little plastic-packed globules reminded Ajay of the crimson cricket balls back in Jamshedpur, of the pitches that shaped him into the competitive engine he is today. He's never had a sweet tooth, but he'd figured there'd be some good omen in coupling transpacific nostalgia with an image of the purest and oldest version of his spirit of ambition. That, and (2) to use the bathroom, where the result of his citric acid and stimulant ingestion has been pee of a dull and troubling copper hue.

In hopes of combatting the poison cocktail, Ajay has been pounding icewater — oceans of it, though at this point more cube than liquid. But he can't seem to ameliorate his drymouth or the debilitating headache that hasn't dissipated since he was loading into Brokenhardt's ages ago. Indeed, Ajay has lost all sense of the passage of time, here, in the too-small apartment, where his sensory intake consists entirely of:

- S.P.L.I.T. figures and deliverables, reflected in sans serif
- twenty browser tabs' project management software industry research
- graphs to indicate
  - o profits
  - o projections
  - o product offerings

The sole plug back into any semblance of Ajay's circadian norm is the digital ticker in the corner of "his" work computer, whose purpose, set in reverse, is to remind him of the minutes counting down to the start of the workday. That and the sun, which began to rise half an hour ago.

Thus unable to work any longer, Ajay emails the slide deck to Angela; appends a brief, chipper message conveying his enthusiasm to present it today; and returns to the bathroom, this time to disrobe and run the bath.

A cold shower ought to baptize him into presentability for Angie's review — and scrub the energy-drink-induced sweat from his glands. Ideally the cleanse will wake him more fully, too. He hasn't felt fully alert since early Tuesday.

Ajay stands under the icy water for several minutes, rubbing his eyes. Then he:

- turns it off
- dresses
- packs "his" work computer into the backpack
- takes a look in the foyer mirror to ensure he doesn't appear too haggard or deranged from a sleep debt he's been machine-gunning with guarana for a long, harrowing, data-driven night and a half

Sure, his ocular bags are pronounced, but he can put on a brave face today. He's done it a million times before. A white lie ("I'm good to keep going!") is a baseline requirement for adulthood.

Ajay dons his boots and winter coat and steps outside toward his crossover, shivering and rubbing his hands together. It's almost 8:30 a.m. Ordinarily he and Angie would've already been catching up since 7:45, but today she has "allowed" him to clock in at nine so he could focus on putting the presentation together.

S.P.L.I.T.-bound, he puts the car in drive.

Ajay is partway finished with the last of the bodega tallboys when he steps into the company office. The building's interior is ominously still in the absence of Fred and of additional fallen soldiers whom S.P.L.I.T. leadership above Ajay's pay grade have recently let go.

Stationed in his hexagonal cube, Ajay fears his tired eyes appear a little too bloodshot. Then he remembers such an image could easily be chalked up to hypertension, which, while not his fault — not that Angie or others would ask; they'd only think him unwell — portends greater trouble for his health. At least that's less incriminating than the energy-drink-infused all-nighter stretching from Wednesday to Thursday, whose cracked-out residual toll of paranoia has him feeling guilty, almost. His thoughts are skirting in fragments — cryptic, out of order, like crossword clues, a negative patina, the opposite of an old glow he hasn't experienced in several years. Too busy. He pictures the tail ends of his dendrites withering and shudders.

Angie hasn't responded to his slide deck email, so Ajay nurses the final tallboy throughout the day, chipping away nervously at project work and waiting for the motion to head upstairs and give her the internal version of his presentation. A short response would have been reassuring, but she hasn't sent one.

Now it's half-past two somehow, the sun is already going down, and Ajay continues to rely on small bouts of adrenaline and whatever drams of guarana and other amines are still coursing through his veins to keep him partially alert. At long last, with the chime of a little digital bell, the email appears. It's an Angie Miller classic: *come upstairs* — no body text, no punctuation. Concerningly, it's not a reply to the slide deck he enclosed this morning; rather, a new chain. Per usual, Ajay has no choice but to heed its instructions.

When he enters Angie's office, her face, for the first time in his memory, almost evinces an expression. It looks negative, but he can't tell anymore. He finishes the energy drink and sets the empty container on the desk dividing them.

"Did you get to take a look at the presentation?" he manages, his voice cracking in a bad blend of poorly feigned eagerness and utter exhaustion.

"Ajay," she says. This is the first time she's gotten his name right. "You're being let go."

Ajay's first thought is that Angie must've seen his name spelled out correctly on just enough human resources paperwork since his hire eight years ago, on digital scraps, on performance reviews and whatever else, for it to finally settle in now. His second thought is of his chest pain, of last night's and today's sears of angina he was certain would let up once the stress of the S.P.L.I.T.-Coldwell merger was over. He's so drained now he can't read his own body, can't discern whether the pain persists.

There's nothing he can say, really, except, "What about the presentation?"

"I haven't gotten to it," she says. "Between the merger itself and making severance decisions, I've been socked in." She pauses. "I'm sorry, Ajay."

"It's okay," he says, then sort of wishes he hadn't. But what good would a concession do anyway? It's too late. Angie is moving too quickly, the merger is moving too quickly, his thoughts are moving too quickly, yet his reactions are so slow.

But maybe there's tranquility in futility. He can take relief in not having a choice.

Angie is saying something. "Do you have any questions for me?"

Between two things — his self-training to speak carefully, especially in code-switchy environments like the S.P.L.I.T. complex, and his all-consuming fatigue — Ajay is beset with a verbal paralysis he knows all too well. His neurons are pinballs trapped in a machine back at the Eisberg-owned arcade of his youth, stuck on "multi-life" — a setting that *seemed* like a windfall but was just the opposite. This "bonus round" introduced only further panic, sending the set of metal orbs careening everywhere and against one another, leaving the player with no objective beyond survival through attrition. One could forestall the end of their turn through increasing desperation — by hammering one's pair of flippers spasmodically against the inevitable downward dual forces of gravity and time. In Ajay's case, the result this morning is a corporate aphasia.

"No," he says.

"I'd still like to use your presentation to prepare things with the Coldwell higher-ups," Angela says. "You can work through the end of this week, and you can answer any of my questions later this afternoon or tomorrow."

There's a long pause. Something inside Ajay is screaming. He has a strong desire, almost a physical urge, to express his shock, his indignation, at this blindsiding insult to incurable injury. Angie and her bosses will appropriate several weeks of his hard work, his stress, just before cutting him loose. His loyalty has been discarded, disregarded.

Were he alone in here, and if Angie's table wasn't secured firmly to the floor beneath it, and if there would be no damages or consequences, Ajay might flip over the faux marble divider between them and hurl it against a wall. He could take a cricket bat to that odious corporate whiteboard, or pelt her computer screen with S.P.L.I.T. darts until it cracks down the middle and the fissures spiral outward like patterns in a frozen pond. He could simply punch or shoulder a hole in the drywall. But he can't process at the right speed for anything useful.

He hears himself saying, "Okay."

"There's some cleaning fluid down in the basement, in the cabinets, under the counter."

Ajay tries not to stare blankly, gears in his mind turning slowly, the insides and outsides of his eyes and synapses desiccating in real time. Her mention of surface spray takes him back, for a moment, to that liminal period at his last gig: Oliver's surface-scrubbing just before Ajay's failure at Brokenhardt's. How long ago was that? Yesterday? Two days ago? A decade?

"For your desk," she clarifies. "They're next to the dartboard." For the first time in their entire working relationship, Angela smiles. "You never spent much time down there, did you?"

"No."

Angie nods her approval. "I've always appreciated that about you. It's just — now there's not enough of that stuff to go around. The money, I mean."

Automatically somehow, Ajay feels the word *redundancy* in his chest. He imagines qualifying it to someone else, the harmless pair of "D" consonants tucked in the middle and issued gently in a Hindi accent, softening the blow. *We go to work to make money*, Angie's voice echoes. Then something occurs to Ajay: some people go to work to help others, to serve the world around themselves, to use their training to take them further in a life of meaning than to administer services like project management software from one business to another. By now, many years into a life of labor, Ajay can claim a comprehensive set of credentials in all kinds of rudiments — software, leadership, social conventions, drums — and a background inextricable from the fiercest work ethic he has ever clocked in anyone else.

Angie has resumed speaking. "Well, Ajay, thank you for everything you've accomplished and contributed here. Not just with the merger recently but throughout the last eight years." She stands, and Ajay stands, too. They shake hands. "You're young," she adds. "You're going places."

Ajay nods, muted. He's been "going places" his entire life — back and forth his whole childhood across the cricket pitch; from bifurcated Bihar over the sea to Chicago; from Raja's house to the Eisberg-owned arcade and back, trailing behind Ira. Then, more recently, up and down treacherous stairwells for dozens — hundreds — of freelance gigs: Dee's residency, Håvi's unsettling groves, the Brokenhardt's disaster. Not too long ago, going places like Genuine Failures, snare case and cymbal bag and corporate backpack in tow, every item weighing him down.

For the last time, head pounding, depleted, Ajay exits Angie Miller's office. He descends to the basement, where two men, younger than he — boys, really — are taking one another on in darts, whooping and cursing and already tucking into their afternoon pale ales. He doesn't recognize them. Maybe it's their American-born privilege, maybe it's the seven or eight years they can enjoy before they reach Ajay's age, or maybe they're here from Coldwell, recent hires, recruiting scouts, whatever — but their presence makes him silently, desperately angry. Perhaps it's a good thing Ajay and S.P.L.I.T. are parting ways. He can admit this resentment, can't resist it, even through the fog, the shock, if only to himself. These people down here — like Ira, like Fred — are careless. Everyone around Ajay is careless. Angie was careless in removing him from the company. That was her mistake. And carelessness isn't endemic to S.P.L.I.T., couldn't possibly be. Blithe, lazy, entitled: some combination of the three can be found in the people who make up any office, every workplace, every leadership position, as far as Ajay knows. A hallmark of working life, isn't it? To be surrounded by people who *care less* than you do, until you retire or die. So, too, in every tragic corner of Chicago, of Illinois, of the United States, of the whole planet. He thinks of that album again, another failure: Mae, whoever she is — the singer who never showed up to Håvi Håvsstrom's studio to make her own record. Careless.

Once back on the main floor of the S.P.L.I.T. office, Ajay doesn't make a show of cleaning out his now-old desk. Ever defensive about embarrassment, he doesn't want anyone paying attention to his departure, desires no sentiment from his farewell. He wouldn't get that validation or meaning from someone else anyway. Still — lifelong, he's been unable to get it from himself.

Hours after its ingestion, the chemical reuptake from Angie's little white pill has Ajay feeling like an automaton. Or maybe this place, the sterile labor environment and "cognitive workplace design" of S.P.L.I.T., has pushed him into behaving like a robot in a competitive and clinical role that goes back far longer than his habit with the tablet. More likely, over the years, even his whole life, some self-pressure has winnowed Ajay's personality into hyper-function.

Or maybe it all dovetails here: the need to "make it" in the United States — to survive — has swallowed up, or forced Ajay to repress, something greater inside himself. Somewhere within him, there must be a force more significant, more meaningful, than a project management role at a software company. Nasally inhaling incidental ambient snits of citrus mist as he wipes down the surface, Ajay feels a fleeting solidarity with Oliver, whom he'll never see again, not unless he returns to Brokenhardt's, which seems 0% likely. He shoves a wad of paper towels into the trash bin below the old desk. Then, quietly, he hauls a stapler, blank papers, old cables, and the laptop — blinking machine, palladium albatross, cursèd thing — to the kitchenette. He leaves it in a cardboard box labeled in thick ink, black blots which are meant to look permanent but aren't. It's a slipshod cemetery for old hardware, a container that's been spilling further and further over with old personal computers as more and more of the S.P.L.I.T. contingent is laid off. A little weight lifts: the office supplies are someone else' problem now.

For the last time, Ajay removes his coat from the spine of his office chair and dons it. For the last time, he trudges from S.P.L.I.T. headquarters' front door to his crossover, and, for the last time, he commutes from the hive of project management software to his too-small apartment. He doesn't listen to music on the way home; it's demanding all his focus simply to stay awake. Part of him is already concerned with what to do next. One must earn a living, of course, but he can still get out of the corporate game, salvage what's left of his heart from the hardening of the last eight years. The inkling of something good occurs to him. But it can wait. Right now, he can only think of sleep.

When Ajay finally returns to his too-small apartment, he fishes Angie's little white pill from the old breast pocket and flicks it into the toilet bowl. Then there's only one thing left to do, one final spurt of taurine and unnatural food dye guiding him before he faceplants the bed, and it won't take long, because he doesn't own a lot of clothing. He rifles through every pants pocket, turns over the sweatshirts in his closet and on his bedroom floor, but it's nowhere to be found. He knows it's not in the car; and if it's stowed for good in a cabinet corner of his now-old desk at the office, even better. Turning the last compartment of his backpack inside out and feeling nothing, Ajay is awash with relief. His talisman, the Seal of Approval® joystick, is gone.

Ajay notices something else as his head hits the pillow for a days-overdue slumber, for, at long last — for the first time in years — peace. He retraces his somatic memory, his tension, physical and mental, the chokehold of paranoia, finally ebbing now... and yes, he's sure of it: the moment Angie Miller dismissed him from her office, his chest pain disappeared.

February 21<u>ˢᵗ</u> (a Wednesday)
Mae

Facing each other on the couch, we're cross-legged in the den upstairs — Ingrid's turf, and a more appropriate place, dead center in the Strand "family" home, for the mother-daughter heart-to-heart I assumed would never happen.

"When?" is all I can think to ask. Ingrid can make her own interpretation.

When were you a songwriter?

When did you work in the music business?

And, most importantly,

When were you going to tell me?

"I was never a success," she says finally.

Aware of this truth but not understanding the specifics, I will Ingrid silently to explain.

She sighs. "Nineteen eighty-seven."

Very, very slowly, I shrug.

"That's when the single came out."

"Okay... that song 'Sugarcoat'?"

"The one," she says. "A full album came afterward, in nineteen eighty-eight. Self-titled. When I was exactly your age."

"An *album*?" I am dumbfounded. "You were... twenty?"

She nods. "Barely old enough to have a handle on what I was doing. But plenty young enough to have ambition. And the promise of a future. The industry, the appeal, my silly adolescence."

"...industry." Head spinning, this, in my incredulity, is the part I end up repeating.

"Not fame, exactly, but... influence. I'm sure you've heard this in your music business classes, but in the eighties, an official album release meant pulling off something a little harder than it is to do now. It was very grand, back then, in terms of reach. Audience. Someone funding things. Artists in my world didn't make and promote albums all by themselves." The lower half of her face contorts into a pained smile. "*Our*selves."

"An ocean of noise," I recite slowly. This is Professor Stuart Hudson Jackson Margolis' term for the modern artist's "competitive landscape." *Innumerable contemporaries*, he'd said.

"I had a career," Ingrid tells me, "for five short years before the album."

"You were fif*teen*?"

"It wasn't wildly young to be making that type of pop music. Probably still is, but I wouldn't know. I think people can tour that young. It's not unheard of. After all, the whole point was for teenagers to relate to it."

"*Tour*?" I cannot, for the life of me, picture Ingrid on stage. I cannot envision her traveling. I cannot even imagine her in a business meeting (in, what, L.A.? New York? London?), participating in the planning of such things. Maybe there were airplanes. Giant buses. Compared to the present, everything about the eighties — the hair, the drums, the fiscal boom — has always seemed so much bigger to me.

"Nothing to get carried away with, baby. I was a supporting act. I didn't have a hit. Not that we didn't try. But that sugarcoat song didn't make it far. I was supposed to *develop* as an artist, make some money for the label, but... the full-length flopped. My debut, I mean. They shelved it almost immediately. The album was supposed to be all deep and confessional and risky. It took me years to prepare, create, record, finesse... and then the industry hated it. Critics tore it apart. That was the final straw, those reviews. The press people who did it were so insecure. A small number of resentful writers — that's all it took. They were never part of the studio magic, so they saw themselves on the margins, and I guess they wanted me to feel like an outsider, too. This one journalist, Barry something, he couldn't stand himself for never really adding to the culture. He wanted to drag the artists down with him. Then people just forgot about the album, which hurt even more. Even the distribution company called it a *regret*.

"And the whole point was that the music and lyrics of that album were supposed to show people what I'd learned when I was searching my soul. What I'd found within myself, what I could bring back up to the surface and share with them. That's why it was self-titled. *Ingrid Lyon*. And so I couldn't help but take all that negative feedback as some indictment of me personally."

She shrugs. "So, yeah, the album tanked. And as a result, I disappeared. That part was easy, actually. It's what the label wanted anyway. At least we agreed on that." She gestures around the living room, her decadeslong hiding place. "I didn't tour again. Obviously. Didn't release anything either. I couldn't bear the risk of another embarrassment. Plus, no one would have supported me."

Wholly stunned, I can only manage a few syllables. "...Lyon."

"I had a name before Strand, you know. Before Erik came into my life. And 'Lyon' had a nice ring to it. The label liked it. Nice imagery."

"You're talking *way* more than normal, Mom."

"Baby, I just heard you sing one of my songs from thirty-five years ago. Big thing. I mean, you singing around the house at all lately — wow." She smiles wanly. "Sugar rush."

"Hiding," I repeat from something she'd said earlier. I'm having trouble believing a musician on the pop spectrum, even at Ingrid's low level of celebrity, could totally disappear. I was brought up in the digital age, though. Maybe they can. My ideas of prior decades, of what was doable, all come from images from TV and movies.

"Vanishing from the public... that might seem difficult to you," she says, reading my mind as only a mother can. "But it wasn't. Think about it: people forget so easily what's kept them entertained. Lyrics, band names, quotes, actors, entire TV shows. All the time. Even the good ones. Slinking away from the career I almost had, from just one horrific album, when everyone involved agreed that I should turn invisible after it failed... it wasn't a tall order in the industry. There's always enough other stuff out there to wash over it."

That phrase, *an ocean of noise*, flits through my mind again.

Continuing to gape, I feel an anger creep up within me, but I don't yet understand why.

"It's like one of those sand mandalas," she continues. "So intricate. So beautiful. It takes those monks hours and hours and hours to put them together. Full days. Weeks, maybe, I don't know. Tiny grains of sand, practiced for years, painstakingly laid down, and then, in a flash, it's all..." She brings her slender fingers down to the couch cushion and runs them together across it. "...brushed away."

"Wait a second," I say, my fury snapping into place, voice shaking: "*This* is why you've been pushing me so hard. Obsessing over music school. Making me make this album. You're — you're *using* me to accomplish something you could never do for yourself."

Ingrid bobs her head from side to side, like she can't quite decide whether that's true. "I suppose it might feel like that to you," she grants finally. "But that's not exactly it. I just... I mean, you are a lot like me." She pauses. I can nearly hear her say, *a better version of me*, or *a more successful version of me*. But she just looks at me like she expects me to agree with her.

"*I am my own person.*"

"You shouldn't waste your abilities, baby. I've been trying to make you understand that since you were a child."

"I'm not *wast*ing anything. I *like* to sing. I just don't like performing. Or doing exercises. Or recording. Well, I guess I don't even know about recording yet. I just — I do it for myself." I fold my arms. "Yeah. I do it for myself."

"Sweetheart, you just don't like working."

Leaving it to Ingrid to correct me again, I throw my hands up in exasperation. "Fine! Maybe I don't like working. Is that so bad? Does everything need to have a *goal*post? What's it all *for*, anyway? Glory? Money?"

Ingrid opens her mouth, maybe to argue or respond — certainly not, if history is any indicator, to soothe or encourage me. Just then, I hear the front door unlocking and swinging open. Robert's home.

"I heard raised voices from in here," he says as he sets down his valise in the entry. And instead of asking, *is everything all right*, he chooses to lead with this: "Did someone say 'money'?"

After a beat, Ingrid, still languid, declares, "Well, the cat's out of the bag."

Robert frowns. "How's that?"

"Nineteen eighty-seven, Robert. Eighty-eight. She knows."

"Ah, well," Robert shrugs. "She was going to find out eventually."

"I'm right here," I remind them hotly. "Wait — *you* were involved back then, too?"

Robert looks at Ingrid, who shrugs with a *you might as well tell her*. "Well, sure," he says. "I wasn't there to support with the actual album, or with your mother's career on that label. Integrity Global, that's what they were called. But right afterward. Helping her disappear." He chuckles. "Sort of an *anti*-career, I suppose."

"And then, what, a few months ago, you just... found her again?"

"When I heard your voice at Grimm's at the start of your semester, I recognized it right away. Pop culture may have let Ingrid Lyon fall by the wayside, but she's unforgettable to me." He directs an expression of something like romance at my mother, and I feel a justified surge of nausea.

"So you heard money in my voice because it echoed hers?"

I'm trying to insult Robert, but it's not working: he seems to be agreeing with me. "The age gap between you two made sense. Her motherhood, I mean. Seeing 'Strand' on your paperwork only confirmed it." He smirks. "Not many people kept a tab on Erik in that period up to his *tragic* passing all those years ago, but I did."

My mind replays that terrifying vignette from my childhood imagination: an upright piano careening downward from twenty stories up, pulpifying Erik in a gruesome death. I look up from my spot on the couch to Robert's wolfish, conniving smile. I stare at him in horror. "Oh my god — Erik — you didn't — " I can't say the word aloud, but I manage to mouth it: *murder.*

Robert and Ingrid meet eyes and burst out laughing. "God, honey, no," Ingrid says. "I loved your father. His death was an accident."

Robert receives a harsh glare from Ingrid when he tells me, "Try to keep up." Is she finally taking my side, even for a moment? Then she continues:

"Anyway, when Erik and I fell in love back then, he helped me evaporate in just the way I wanted. He was more than willing to move to suburban Illinois and raise you in peace and quiet. I met him at just the right time. He liked me for who I was — not for my *potential* or even for my talents."

"I wish you felt that way about me."

Ingrid sucks in her breath. "If it makes you feel any better, Erik was happy to let me take control of your musical development, nudge you into lessons, push you to practice. Or at least try. For those first fifteen years, he just clocked into his nine-to-five and supported us. I had tiny chunks of royalties from that 'Sugarcoat' single and from a few music videos. Next to nothing. Our unremarkable little life. And he let me curl up here, didn't mind my exhaustion, never held my sadness against me. My life felt like an accident I couldn't control. Awful luck, Erik..."

"You're a ghost," I burst. "A *ghost*" — and here I move on to Robert — "and *you're* just here to monetize me. Us. You probably don't even want to help Ingrid with her — this awful dream — bringing her voice back to life, using mine, so I can make something permanent, or successful, where she fell short. Or if you do, you just want to sleep with her."

At this, Robert says nothing. Neither does Ingrid.

"Well, that'll work out perfectly," I conclude, out of breath, quaking, unfolding my legs and sinking into the couch. "All she does is sleep anyway."

There's a moment of silence.

"Well," says Ingrid softly, "where does that leave us?"

I never thought my mother would put decisionmaking onto me — not on my life. I've never imagined how I might reply to such a question. After all, I figured the prompt would never come. But the answer is simple.

"I want to do music for *me*," I tell them.

Ingrid looks at Robert, who appears to be leaving the response up to her. He's looking back at my mother with a clement half-smile. Maybe this benevolence, something I've never seen in him before, is something he reserves for her.

"That's fair," she says ultimately.

"No more *goals*," I say. "No more album. No more obsession with my singing becoming influential, or important, or recognized, or public, or whatever. If I want to sing, I'll do it for myself. In the basement, maybe. Or in the shower." This scores a small laugh from the pair of them. I look especially hard at Robert. "And if you actually like her for her — Ingrid for Ingrid — I guess I can stomach your being around."

Robert nods. I don't detect sarcasm or irony. He's said what he's said, and so have I, and promises are just that — promises. Maybe Robert and

I will each walk away with the same private revelation: we both don't need to lie quite so much.

"I guess you'll have to tell Håvi the album is off, then," I continue. "Not that we got much done anyway."

Robert nods again. "I'll tell him."

"What's the deal with that guy, anyway?"

Robert and Ingrid look at each other.

"We should just send her that page," he says.

"What page?" I ask.

"There's a Canonymous entry no one ever reads," Robert says. "But the website admin won't let us have it taken down. They're fixated with *historical integrity*. Art and entertainment. Cultural memory. So they won't delete it." He shakes his head. "Packrats. We've even tried emailing the moderator, but they insist on keeping the data out there."

Silently, I will him to spell it out.

"The page is for Ingrid," he says. "For her one album."

"But it gets only maybe three or four views a year," Ingrid adds. "It sort of just... exists. The only visits are from us."

"She refreshes it every six months or so, just to see whether it's still there. And sometimes she goes through the whole thing, just to chew on it, when she's depressed."

How sad, how aggravatingly predictable, that Robert would acknowledge my mother's low states of mind without offering to help. I mull on how weird this all is: the quiet tragedy of Ingrid's life.

"Yeah, send it to me."

Ingrid stands up. She lifts one hand, queenlike, inviting me to stand up, too. The moment feels unnatural until my mother steps toward me and wraps me wordlessly into an enormous, comfortingly tight, Mae-enveloping hug. It's the first time she's embraced me in years.

February 23rd (a Friday)
Ajay

For his entire adulthood, every pivotal moment in Ajay Chadhana's life has been followed immediately by the need to sit down, crack his knuckles, and hammer out a good email.

First, though, after the layoff, he'd slept for thirty-six hours straight. Entirely free of fitfulness, of subconscious intrusion — physically still — Ajay finally got the rest he really, really needed.

It's now Friday afternoon, and, stretching his limbs, yawning and fixing himself darjeeling, Ajay thinks about the email to come. In this case, actually, there will be two of them. He would have sent the first one early last week if it hadn't been for the stress of the merger. Now that harrowing engagement feels so long ago, and so starkly impersonal, it feels like it was hanging over his head in another life. In a way, it was.

He opens an unwritten reply to that most recent correspondence from his biological mother, her lengthy note from nearly two weeks ago. He doesn't populate it with any text — not yet. He won't today. Premeditation is better. Omission will be helpful, i.e., withholding that he's been let go from his longtime employer. His mother doesn't need to know his elimination was S.P.L.I.T.'s decision. All she needs to know is — what? He should decide for himself before divulging, before defending or explaining his choices. How about this: he'll say he's decided to move on from software project management. Of his own accord. He wants to do something good in the world. He's elected to open the suite of possibilities in his life beyond a position as middling corporate leader. The implications about fiscal stability, about prestige, might shock her, but his mother needs to accept his self-determination. Only in the last hour has he started to accept this autonomy for himself.

The kettle whines while Ajay turns over the specifics of the response to come. He'd like to articulate a note of forgiveness, but he can't quite wrangle the idea. He wants to extend *pardon* to his mother, absolution, but any gnawing ideas — what transgressions, exactly? — are all too broad to describe or resolve today. Pre-vindication, it will take time to dig further into the heart he's felt warming alongside the tea leaves this afternoon. Anyway, it was her pushiness, her intensity, that informed his survival in the United States, facilitated and even guided it, from across an ocean. So an attending admission of Ajay's own gratitude would be well-placed, too, and in step with a softer and more sensitive soul. But does she even think something is broken between them? Is it only he that stews on it? He's reluctant to ask, and email (though Ajay loves a cathartic email) may not be the best platform for that conversation. Best to wait until the next time he visits Jamshedpur, but that might be a few years from now. So he'll invest the time in thinking harder before their next video call.

Ajay conducts a little purge in his browser, and he feels even more weight falling from his shoulders. All twenty of the tabs — flush with hypertension research, indicating personal risks for myocardial infarction and assessing other vascular chronic conditions or nascent physiological crises for South Asians — deleted. *Let go*, Angela might say, though with a much more distasteful implication on her part. No bookmarks, no cookies. Just gone, and gone completely. They vanished with his old job, his old position, his old duality.

Then he opens another tab, one whose results will help him finish that first email and its psychological topics with his mother well into the future. More importantly, though, it will help Ajay with himself. The search:

184

therapists south asian chicago

He can almost hear his elders, biological and adoptive alike, inquiring into the therapist's academic qualifications — where did they obtain their Master's degree? undergraduate? what about a doctorate? — but no matter: Ajay can judge their credibility for himself.

Enjoying this momentum, Ajay sets that search aside for later today and opens a third new email, whose impetus occurred to him just after waking up today — as if in a dream, though its possibilities are very real and very exciting. Will its consequences tie together this in-between field in life, this pivot point before his next office job? A placeholder while he seeks other long-term vocations that might foster something good in this world, while he explores what that might mean? He can't say just yet, and for the first time in Ajay's life, he has a blank space before him and a firmer idea of what he can use to fill it, and that feels nice. Private enthusiasm is pleasant and new. Let it simmer.

The instigator had appeared just before that nightmare at Brokenhardt's. Milling around the basement floor, Ajay had noticed a flyer among many other punk goings-on and events on the corkboard in the stairwell. He may not have clocked the little cardstock rectangle if loading drums into the venue didn't involve so many trips, didn't encourage second glances at his surroundings where other artists or patrons only got one cursory look heading in. Inundated with stressors at the time, he'd filed its invitation incredibly far back in his mind. But now the opportunity, realistic for the first time, is what he's sure he wants to pursue — and, based on his qualifications, and his newfound eagerness to improve the world (or at least Chicago), he's credentialed to get there.

Ajay pulls open the institution's website to retrieve the office administrator's email address. He taps out the subject line to the third message and begins to type.

Seeking Position: Drum Instructor at Grimm's Academy

February 21<u>ˢᵗ</u> (a Wednesday)
Mae

SELF-TITLED (Ingrid Lyon album) (1988) (Ultra-rare)

Ingrid Lyon's eponymous album, Lyon's final release and "most difficult" listen[citation needed], was released September 13, 1988, via Integrity Global Records.[1] A commercial failure, *Ingrid Lyon* was received unfavorably by fans and critics alike[2] and has been identified retroactively as having put an almost immediate end to Lyon's then-growing artistic and public profile. The album — Lyon's first full-length — was produced by Håvi Håvsstrom, who once described his decision to work on the LP as "one of the few regrets of [his] career."[3]

The first and only single, "This Sugarcoat," whose lyrics address pet cemeteries with unsettling specificity[4], garnered functionally no radio attention with the exception of several "novelty rotations"[5] in Lyon's hometown of Chicago and, according to the era's admittedly rudimentary media monitoring aggregators, fewer than ten broadcasts in New York and Los Angeles on the day of its release. The single obtained no airplay — at least that we Canonymous volunteers could discern — internationally or in American cities of sub-Chicago population density. [6] Upon its release, the track was pinpointed by Integrity Global Records CEO Blaine Steppssen (who, true to his surname, had inherited the international distributor from his stepfather Ricky in 1981) as, for Lyon's trajectory as a vocalist, creative force and projected font of revenue for I.G.R., "the quick start of the even quicker end."[7]

Background

In an effort to "break completely free of the pop constraints" that had theretofore defined her career — the 7" single explicated above, and two music videos[8] — Lyons [*sic*] has stated she began putting together "various incarnations" of the *Ingrid Lyon* record during the period spanning 1982-1987, beginning when she was a teenager. [9] Lyon's expressed ambition was to create, record and release a landmark album that would challenge listeners' expectations and serve as her most deeply psychological and self-investigative.[10] In a *Retrospector* review posted at the time of its release and titled "The Sweet Limelight Glow, In the End, Shall Fail Without Natural Sucrose," pop/ rock journalist Barry Citron excoriates the results:

> "On a platter of sweeping guitars, glittery synths, and reverb-gated snares, Ingrid Lyon's sensibilities and imagination served her smallish pack of acolytes, and casual pop listeners, with the very finest candy... until now [1988]. Sure, the material was generic, but it was saccharine, dammit, and it was meted to us in deliciously, delightfully small doses. And so Ms. Lyon's devoted little fanbase, and an even smaller cadre of critics, swallowed the singles and the footage with ease.
>
> Perhaps, unfortunately for her, our neon decade's most self-aggrandizing twelve-gauge plastic dispenser of confessional bitter pills constitutes hard proof that Ms. Lyon — if I.G.R. permits her to continue

recording and releasing music — ought to stick to confectionary fiction... wrought and compounded, as we have come to expect from Ingrid and her team, in its most anodyne chemical form."[11]

Writing for <u>Knock Turn</u> in 1988, in "Ingrid? More Like Off-Grid," Ray Carmel submits his own unflinching assessment:

"In her increasingly infrequent interviews with *Knock Turn* leading up to the release of her somewhat highly anticipated full-length debut, Ingrid Lyon has described the artistic motivation behind the effort — now nearly guaranteed to be her last — as 'an elaborate act of self-destruction.' Career-wise, and at only twenty, she's certainly proven this statement to be true. Cresting a staggering and unpleasant 70 minutes, the scope of *Ingrid Lyon*, and its impact on the listener, is nothing short of cruel and unusual. Too, its subject matter — at once maudlin, grandiose, and self-indulgent — divulges, in stark relief, a supernova swelling and collapsing long before reaching its peak brightness. Falling woefully short of delivering on tenacity, the album, declawing itself, settles on boredom."[12]

Carmel concludes: "The most incriminating facet of the album is its eponymity."[13]

Branding

The cover artwork [*no longer accessible in digital or print media*] features a poorly rendered iconograph of Lyon assuming the form of a large felid predator.[14]

<u>Retrospective Analysis</u> *[n/a]*

Since its release, *Ingrid Lyon* (the album) and Ingrid Lyon (the person) have largely evaded the maw of pop-cultural memory. On account of the album's reception, Lyon has given neither Q's nor A's, nor public appearances, from 1988 to present, and we couldn't find any evidence indicating she's been asked to do so.

Owed to Lyon's admittedly meager recognition prior to this final album, self-avowed audiophilic crate-diggers,[15] pop-arts bloggers, and 80's enthusiasts will, in extremely infrequent cases, unearth ultra-limited CD formats of the album only to find it "confusing,"[16] "frightening"[17][18][19][20] and, "probably above Ingrid's pay grade, even if it wasn't above Håvsstrom's."[21]

Personnel and Recording Process

In 1983, then managed and "legally handled" by Integrity Global Records' internal legal team, with attorney Frank Price at the helm,[22] Lyon withdrew from the public eye after returning home from a supporting slot on <u>Jodie Hall</u>'s *Comets and Caterwauls* tour, in which Lyon's participation as an opening act had been coordinated and promoted by I.G.R. in hopes of catalyzing her career.[23] Lyon then elected to hole away from "clamoring fans and fee lines" in an undisclosed location in order to focus on composing her magnum opus.[23.5] Though the nature of Lyon's relationship with Price was unclear (and, due to her failure to survive in media gestalt, journalistic coverage, and general artistic accreditation since the album's release, remains unknown to the public), Lyon stated in 1987 interviews that she attempted to impose a personal and professional distance between herself and Price during the album's making.[24] Lyon also reported she frequently arrived at the studio to find I.G.R. legal and financial representatives and Håvsstrom "already embroiled in deep discussion — without me — every time I appeared in the doorway."[25]

Lyon described the recording process as a "horror"[26][27][28]
[29][30] and reflected that she "spent more time during those
sessions curled up, catlike, fused to a couch in the side
room watching sitcom reruns and baseball [*sic**] than I ever
spent singing or writing songs in my entire life."[31] Made increasingly uncomfortable by the crescendo of intimacy and
privacy between Price' lackeys and Håvsstrom during the
Ingrid Lyon sessions, Lyon quietly hired her own entertainment lawyer, Robert Koenid, "strictly for CYA concerns"[32]
and to forestall legal "factors outside [her] control."[33] Of
Koenid's presence, Lyon also admitted that, "with all that
discomfort and all that free time, it was just nice to have
some company."[34]

In the weeks leading up to its release, when Lyon's self-titled was broached in interviews, Håvsstrom had already
begun to downplay his own involvement in the album,
putatively on the basis of some private embarrassment.
[35] Too, the *Ingrid Lyon* hyperlink has since been removed
from the production discography featured on Håvsstrom's
own Canonymous page. (The digital consulting team
representing Håvsstrom's present-day business affairs
have, arms folded, occluded all possibility of Canonymous'
digital reinstatement. Believe us. We've tried.) Håvsstrom
has also dodged any association with the album's difficult
lyrical content with a carefully scripted reference to his
own loose command of the English language[citation needed]
and a lightning-fast redirection of the conversation to his
extensive roster of otherwise successful work throughout

---

* **Author's note**: Though it meant very little to her, Ingrid Lyon watched India win the 1983
Cricket World Cup as a much-needed distraction in real time during her escape from fans and
press after the *Comets and Caterwauls* tour the year prior. During this time, Lyon prepared for
her opus-to-come by "getting some thinking done" via the heavy ingestion of cable television
and of what she referred to as "catnip."

Four years later, while seeking refuge from the nascent exclusive relationship between
Håvsstrom and Price during the *Ingrid Lyon* sessions, Lyon watched a second flagship Cricket
World Cup — the 1987 series, hosted by India and Pakistan — the first, notably, to be held
outside the United Kingdom.

190

the 1980's, 1990's, 2000's, and 2010's, in bubblegum pop, new wave, alternative rock, and EDM.[36][37][38][39][40][41][42]

February 22<u></u>nd (a Thursday)
Mae

Ingrid is driving the Strand-Koenid "family" vehicle. Actually, from now on, let's just call it the Strand vehicle. I'm in the shotgun seat. The two of us haven't ridden together one-on-one in a long time. I'm told we barely used the old car after Erik died. It just sat dormant at the house for about a decade, not unlike the person who inherited it, until Ingrid and I agreed, for school and as a budding musician, I should learn how to drive. Given the option of the train, though, I've refrained from getting myself anywhere. Not one for the idea of ownership, I've always preferred the passenger seat.

Though we're in transit, I'm not experiencing that TV script thing right now. I haven't in a while. Even in our typically quiet quarters, life has gotten pretty interesting lately. It's not just that, though: Ingrid herself is interesting. I haven't felt that way about my mother until last night — not because she was once almost famous, but because I know her better now.

She's taking me to this morning's lesson with Emily, which has timed out well after that whole discussion about my singing — my *doing* music — for its own sake. I look forward to it. I always do. I'm not sure how much I'll tell Emily about last night, but I'll make that decision in ten minutes or so. When I see her, I'll know.

Ingrid said she wanted to "get some stuff done outside the house" today, which is a revelation, both parts of it: *get stuff done,* and *outside* the house. During my childhood, she had to leave *some*times; the grocery store, the post office, the doctor, the bank. It's not like a person can give up completely on appearing places. Still, though, in the last year and a half, Ingrid skipped all my Grimm's parent-instructor check-ins, even though they had her best interests at heart. Knowing what I know now, though, I realize showing up at the school may have made Ingrid afraid of being recognized by the pop music alumni who teach there.

"What are you and Emily working on today?" she asks me.

A reflexive scowl starts to form across my face. Habits don't die overnight. I wipe it away before she sees. Thankfully, she's paying attention to the road ahead.

"Sorry," she adds quickly, reading my mind. "I'm not asking you out of pressure, Mayfly. Just... making conversation about your day." She laughs lightly. "I guess we'll both have to get used to that."

"I think it's a good thing," I venture.

Ingrid nods.

There's an awkward beat.

"So what are you — " Both of us ask at exactly the same time, in exactly the same inflection. We laugh, both of us suddenly self-conscious. I really am my mother's daughter. Then she just nods without looking, giving me the go-ahead.

"I was gonna ask what you're up to today," I say, "that's all."

Now she's crafty: "I have... interests of my own."

I imagine Ingrid, inspired by last night's events, in a vocal booth an hour from now, or perhaps in a meeting with a producer or manager. Now that I know about her fascinating past, her alter ego, she could be a superheroine.

"I'm going to start volunteering at the pet shelter downtown," she says. "I'll be picking up their application today and seeing whether they'll take me."

"...that's cool."

"It'll be good for me to have something to do. And put a little good into the world."

"But what if someone recognizes you?"

She shrugs. "They might. They also might not."

It hadn't occurred to me that everything for Ingrid might work out fine.

"Either way," she concludes, once again reverberating my thoughts, "I'll survive."

"You want my advice, Mom? Don't let any pianos fall on your head."

She appears to examine the idea, weighing the possibility. We're a few minutes away from Grimm's, and I have to ask:

"So you — you and Robert..."

She nods, having anticipated this question. "He likes me for me, Mae. I know that might be difficult to understand, but he's seen who I used to be, and who I am now, which is a very rare thing. And he's accepted both of those versions of me."

"I trust your judgment," I tell her, processing and trying to be sympathetic. I wait a moment, then: "But yeah, so he's not like Håvi."

She frowns.

"I feel like Håvi wanted to use people like you," I continue. "People like us. Our voices. But also because both of us weren't in a position to negotiate very much when we were recording with him. He kind of created that world."

"Håvi Håvsstrom isn't *evil*, Mae."

"Well, he's still a jerk."

Though she knows much more about Håvi than I do, Ingrid nods seriously. "You're right, Mae. The way Robert has accepted me, and the way Håvi was interested in me — those are very, very different." She shakes her head. "This business of music. Sometimes it feels like there's no freedom, no pleasure, and no room for family. Also no money. At least the way it happened for me."

I wait for her to continue.

"I'm glad for you, Mae. That's the main thing — the only thing. That you're doing what *you* want to do, and *not* doing what you *don't* want to do. But it's also probably good to see if you can avoid the commercial side of things. I have no idea what the industry is like now anyway."

"People say it's harder than it used to be."

"You can do anything you want to do," she says with intense conviction. "You're my daughter, and I really do believe that. But if music as commerce is making you miserable, or if you were just doing it for me, or for Robert, then there's no pressure to pursue it."

We arrive at the academy parking lot.

"I'm going to head in there and sing," I tell her, "because that's what I'd like to do."

Ingrid beams — really beams, for the first time I've seen in my life. I unbuckle my seatbelt, lean over, and give her the best side hug I can manage. She squeezes me. Her tenderness and sincerity, which I've been craving for years, transcend the awkward angle and the console between us.

"I'll pick you up when you're done," she says.

I'll pick you up when you're done. That promise, I think, indicates a bright future for us. That wherever I land, whichever way things go, my mother will pick me up. There can be mutual trust. This is Ingrid's brilliant exhale to the past we endured apart — each of us, until now, lonely under the same suburban roof. I open the door, wave Ingrid a gentle morning goodbye, and exit the vehicle, backpack slung over one shoulder.

ACKNOWLEDGEMENTS

Front cover, back jacket and spine illustrations by Bri Smejkal, the most important person in my world.

Unspectacular would not have been possible without:

Niki Gjoni, for her extraordinary professional developmental editing;

Carolyn, Nick, Eric, Isaiah, and Andy, for their unflinching feedback on early drafts;

Hennepin County Library, for offering functionally limitless contemporary fiction, literary classics, cultural histories of cricket, and patience with me; and

Christian, for once gently suggesting: "Make your prose sound more like you."

The dozens of bandmates who have populated my world for a decade and taught me everything.

My family, for setting their goals unreasonably high so I could one day do the same.

ZAQ BAKER

Ranging from the quirky to the desperately serious, Zaq Baker dares to ask what might happen if a writer trapped in a pianist's body jumped around from pop-punk to synth-rock to modern pop to musical theatre.

Accolades from 2024: "All We Wanted Was a Gem that Wouldn't Fade" is featured in new film *How to Break a World Record*. Zaq shared the keynote speaking and performing role at Youth Mental Health Day, a 730-attendee-strong weeklong nonprofit symposium; captained Zaq Baker Team at Art-a-Whirl music festival's Liquid Zoo; and was musical guest on *Minnesota Tonight!*, a longstanding talk show. Most importantly, his Instagram stories have been re-shared by Boy Meets Girl, U-Haul, La Croix, Grainbelt, The Academy Is..., and two acclaimed Minneapolis restaurants.

Zaq has been co-writing a musical, *Hometown*, since 2022.

In addition to his eponymous work, Zaq is a full-time member of pop-rock quintet Maria and the Coins; synth-punk sextet Toilet Rats; indie vocalist pop outfit Corzine; Poison Ivy And The People; Nina Luna's live band; and more. Zaq frequently co-writes with other artists; is a Music Director; writes artist bios and copy for his peers; and contributes piano and keyboards to albums, performances and videos as a freelance session musician.

zaqbaker.com

Instagram: @zaqbaker

Spotify, Apple Music, YouTube, and TIDAL: Zaq Baker

TikTok: @zaqbaker

Made in the USA
Monee, IL
01 February 2025

11389317R00115